Mail Order Grace

Book One of
Mail Order Bluebonnet Brides

Charlotte Dearing

This is a clean, wholesome love story set in late 19th century Texas. The hero is strong, successful, and flawed, in ways he doesn't realize until he meets the heroine. In the end, they find happiness through perseverance and faith.

Chapter One

Grace O'Brian

Grace hurried to the window to look at the street, three stories down. Men shouted at each other. She wiped the frost away with her bare hand, shocked at how cold it was. An early spring storm made it feel like the dead of winter again, and the frigid pane of glass made her shiver.

When men behaved badly, like the two on the street below, it scared Grace. She'd rather not be witness to such behavior. But she was drawn to look, needing to know what the disagreement was about, and to see how things would turn out.

This was not the worst part of Boston, but it wasn't the nicest either. Thugs and pickpockets often roamed the darkened alleys around the boarding house. Just last week, on her way home from the workhouse, she'd been accosted by a hoodlum demanding the wages she'd just been paid. Thankfully, a constable was nearby, and he ran the hoodlum away.

The two men yelled, both poised to fight. They snarled profanities at each other. It was a common scene in this part of Boston, but the vulgar language always shocked her. A crowd gathered, cheering them on.

"Dear Lord," Grace murmured. "I have a train to catch in an hour. How will I get to the station if there's a brawl on our very doorstep?"

Grace's sisters came to her side and stared down with her, neither saying a word. Suddenly one of the men brandished a knife, and the three girls gasped.

Grace knew that, any minute, there could be bloodshed. Cold dread swirled inside her. She turned to her sisters. "Don't watch this spectacle. It isn't good for anyone's nerves. Soon we'll all be in Texas amidst more wholesome folk."

Faith and Hope drew back, nodding in agreement.

Grace wanted to get everyone thinking about something other than the violence happening outside their building.

"Come help me pack the last of my things, and we'll talk about my trip and how long it might be until you can come join me."

Grace wished she could take her sisters with her today. Her trip to Texas, to become a mail-order bride, was a desperate bid to improve their lot in life. Their jobs in the lace factory were not physically demanding, but the strain on their eyes would one day rob them of their sight, and the cold, cold winters in Boston would soon enough rob them of their health.

Two months ago, her youngest sister, Faith, had been stricken with a cough that Grace was sure would take her. For ten days, the cough never let up, and it weakened Faith to the point that Grace was nearly ready to ask their minister to come and say prayers at her bedside. But Faith's cough gradually left her, and her strength slowly returned to the point that, now, if you didn't know Faith, you might not realize that she nearly had gone to her final reward.

The weather today, the twenty-fifth of March, wasn't much better than it had been back in January when Faith fell ill. Grace said a silent prayer that Faith could avoid a spring cold.

Concern for her sisters drove her to make this trip to a place so far away. She might not be the bravest of the O'Brian girls, but she was the eldest. She felt the need to protect them, as best she could.

Faith sat on the far bed, regarding her with wide, tear-filled eyes. Standing by the window, pale and trembling, she stood by her other sister, Hope. Grace tried to give her sister a reassuring smile as she folded her lace work. The three of them had known their share of rough men, starting with their own father. Liam O'Brian had always been a good man, a loving father and husband, but a carriage accident changed all that.

The doctors didn't think he'd survive the wound to his head. After months confined to his bed, he recovered, but was never the same. His moods swung wildly. When angered, he became violent with his wife and daughters. The memory of his fits of rage always made Grace's blood run cold. Her father had passed, but he still appeared in her nightmares every so often.

Dangerous men lurked in the workhouses of Boston, too.

They'd escaped the workhouses unscathed, thank goodness, but all of them silently worried about the dangers present to single young women in Boston. They'd worried about John Bentley too, her future husband in Texas, but Grace sensed kindness in his letters. She trusted that he'd treat her with care. Maybe that was nothing more than wishful thinking, but she decided from the beginning to set those thoughts aside, especially when she learned John had a small child, a little girl whose mother had died after giving birth. The notion of a small, motherless child lent her journey to Texas even greater urgency.

"John Bentley is as fine a man as I'd find in Texas. When I get settled, I promise to send for you as quickly as possible."

"Why must you go early?" Faith asked, her voice barely above a whisper.

"John writes that he's ailing. He won't say why, but as his wife-to-be, it's my duty to care for him. I can't rest knowing he's doing poorly while he tries to care for a young babe."

Faith shook her head mournfully. "Will he be angry that you've come two weeks early?"

Grace tucked her lace shawl into her valise and set the bag atop her traveling trunk. She tried her best to give them a show of bravado. O'Brian women prided themselves on resoluteness. *Better to ask forgiveness than permission.*

Hope wiped her eyes with a handkerchief. "You're traveling all that way to a man you know only through letters. You haven't even said your vows before God."

"It's true. All we have is a signed proxy. John's promised that we'll say our vows in church when I arrive."

A loud crash came from next door. The sound was followed by yelling. The walls muffled the words, but it was clear their landlord argued with his wife. Again. Strife and violence surrounded the three girls. If they didn't encounter it on the street or workhouse, they suffered it here in the boarding house. Sometimes, the landlord and his wife screamed at each other for an hour or more.

Another reason to leave Boston. Their boarding house was one of the better ones in the neighborhood, yet it still had problems. Loud tenants. Leaky pipes. Cold as the North Pole in winter, and hot as a furnace in summer.

"I won't miss Mr. and Mrs. Roberts," Grace said quietly.

She sat down to brush her hair. Faith took the brush from her. "Let me."

The gesture was simple, yet it made Grace's heart squeeze with pain. How she would miss her sisters. Mama and Papa had been gone four years now. Both had passed within a day of each other, Mama from a fever, and Papa of a broken mind and a crushed spirit. When their mother passed, their father lay down in the bed, closed his eyes and died that night.

Grace and her sisters had always been close, but since losing their parents, they clung to each other with even greater affection.

The three girls were close in age. Grace, at twenty-one, was the eldest. Faith was a year younger and Hope just eighteen. The girls all shared the same Irish coloring of their mother, red hair, blue eyes and fair skin. Grace's hair was a deep copper hue, the color of a new penny, while her two sisters had a lighter, golden-red color.

"What will we do without you?" Faith murmured.

"Take good care of each other. That's what you'll do. Stay well. Keep the Sabbath and say your prayers at bedtime."

Faith smiled. "Yes, mother hen."

"Keep your spirits up. That's the best thing for you to do."

Another round of shouting erupted from the room next door. Both Mr. and Mrs. Roberts cursed like sailors. Grace and Faith winced when they caught a few choice words. The bad words always came through loud and clear.

Faith sighed and finished arranging Grace's hair in an elegant twist at the base of her neck. She rested her hands upon Grace's shoulders. Giving her a wistful look, she spoke. "You'll be a beautiful bride."

Hope appeared at her side, holding a small tissue-wrapped package. "We bought something for you."

Grace rose and gave a small huff of surprise. "You shouldn't have."

Faith and Hope grinned at each other. They were a mischievous pair and it made her heart sing to see their faces wreathed in smiles.

She shook her head with mild reproach. "We can't afford gifts."

"Go on, open it," her sisters said in unison.

Grace untied the ribbon and unwrapped the tissue to find a locket and chain. In the dimly lit room, the gold sparkled. She let out a soft cry of surprise.

Faith took the locket and pressed a small notch on the side. When the locket sprang open, Grace saw that it contained two locks of hair. Each lock was tied with a tiny strand of lace.

"You see," Hope said excitedly. "A little piece of us will travel with you all the way to Texas."

"So you won't forget us," Faith added.

Grace knit her brow, feigning indignation. "As if I could!"

Faith took the locket and put it around Grace's neck. Just as she closed the clasp, the church bells rang, signaling that it was noon. Time to go to the train station. Nobody spoke for a long moment, until Grace broke the silence.

"The train leaves soon. I must go."

"We'll all go," Hope exclaimed.

Grace shook her head. "Please let me say my goodbye here. It's cold and damp outside. I couldn't bear the notion of you catching cold because you took me to the train station."

She crossed the room and looked out the window. The hansom cab waited by the front door. Mr. Bentley had sent enough money for her to travel in luxury. The idea was almost too much. No, it *was* too much. After years of pinching pennies and fretting about every expense, she hadn't been prepared for Mr. Bentley's generosity. If anything, it left her wracked with guilt over the extravagance.

The only thing she'd indulged in were some gifts for Mr. Bentley's little girl. She'd bought her a doll and a china tea set. The child was far too young for a china tea set, but Grace hadn't been able to resist. She recalled the day she saw the set in a shop window and had to buy it for Abigail. She'd wrapped the offerings in tissue, packed them carefully, and imagined giving them to the little girl.

Over the weeks and days leading up to her departure, the thought comforted her and pleased her. In her mind, she could almost see the little girl. The yearning she felt to be a mother to the child was every bit as strong as her desperate need to find a new life for her sisters. Especially since the child had never known her own mother.

Grace's sisters came to her side and looked down at the horse and buggy.

"Well, then," said Faith. "At least we can rest assured that Mr. Bentley will take good care of you."

"I think he means to spoil me," Grace said. "He claims he needs to treat me especially well, since his brothers are dead-set against my coming to Texas."

Faith's eyes widened. "My word!"

Grace shook her head. "I shouldn't have said anything. I'm sure it will be fine. Just fine. I'd best go now. I can't keep the driver waiting."

Chapter Two

Matt Bentley

Matthew Bentley gazed at his brother as he lay in his bed. John's stoic features were twisted with pain. For weeks now, his brother battled the rattlesnake bite. John had finally agreed to let the doctor come to his home and examine his leg, but he'd been obstinate about any care the doctor recommended.

Matt tried to rein in his temper. It wasn't easy with a brother like John. His older brother had only gotten more stubborn and set in his ways since he'd lost his wife last year. Matt forced his lips into a polite smile.

"I got a visit from Dr. Phillips this morning."

John lay in the middle of the four-poster bed, in his bedroom in the old family homestead. A sheen of sweat glistened on his brow. He'd soaked his nightshirt already and he'd just put a fresh shirt on after his breakfast. It was clear his brother was burning up with fever. The snake bite had done more damage to John's leg than anyone was willing to admit, especially John.

"You keep that old cuss away from me," John growled.

"He says the leg isn't healing."

"It's fine. I'll be fit as a fiddle by the time we take the cattle to Fort Worth. You watch."

"That's in two days, John."

"I know it's in two days." John's face reddened. "The snake bit my leg, not my head."

Matt gritted his teeth to keep from giving a sharp reply. There was no reasoning with his brother once he made up his mind. He was as stubborn as the day was long.

"You need me on that ride," John muttered.

Matt knew that was true. The Sanders clan was likely to give them trouble on the way to Fort Worth. There was no shortage of bad blood between the Sanders clan and Bentleys.

John continued. "Another pair of eyes. Another gun. Someone to turn a stampede." John tapped his chest. "That would be me, if you recall."

Matt nodded. A cowboy's worst nightmare was a stampede. Panicked cattle could injure or kill each other as well as a horse and rider. He and his brothers had suffered a stampede two years back, just outside of Magnolia. It had happened at night, and there was every reason to believe one of the Sanders family had spooked the cattle. John had managed to turn the stampede. He targeted the lead steer and forced him to turn and slow. Thankfully, the cowboys managed to regain control before any were lost or rustled.

The hard feelings between the Sanders and the Bentleys stemmed from a decades-old argument between men who were long dead. Still, the animosity lingered. The Sanders had come upon hard times. The two brothers, Frank and Jed, despised the Bentley brothers. They'd cause mischief every chance they got.

The nurse came into the bedroom carrying a tray. She gave Matt a pained look. Her shoulders stooped.

"You better be nicer than Doc," John grumbled. "One word about taking off my leg and I'll run you off too."

The nurse nodded. Matt wondered if she didn't look just the least bit hopeful at the prospect of someone running her off. He couldn't blame her. John was impossible when he was well. Sick, injured and bedridden, he was probably the worst patient in all of Magnolia.

She drew the sheet down to reveal John's injured leg. Matt grimaced at the sight. When the doctor said it was getting worse, he wasn't lying. Matt had assumed that John exaggerated about the doctor's comment about amputating his leg. Now he wasn't so sure. John's foot and lower calf were easily twice the size they should be. The puncture wounds on the ankle oozed and the color of his skin varied between a grim shade of purple and an ominous hue of green.

The nurse recoiled.

"Hush now," John growled.

With shaking hands, the young woman cleaned and dressed the wound. John groaned in pain whenever she repositioned his leg. Matt felt sickened to see his older brother in pain. The snake bit him two weeks ago. Each day, John had gotten worse. The snake bite was entirely John's doing. He'd tried to take on a rattler without a tool or weapon. Somehow, John Bentley, a man who lived his entire life on a Texas ranch, tried to kill a three-foot rattler with the heel of his boot.

Bad idea. Just like pretty much all of John's ideas of late.

Matt's thoughts spun with the possibility that John might get worse, or even lose his life. When the nurse left the room, Matt leaned forward in his chair. "You need to write that gal from Boston."

John knit his brow. "What gal from Boston?"

"You don't remember?"

"What are you talking about?"

Matt sat back in the chair and stared at his brother with complete disbelief. For the last two months, the man had spoken about nothing other than the girl he planned to send for. Grace O'Brian was going to be the solution to all his problems. She'd help him mend his broken heart. She'd be a mama to baby Abigail. She'd turn his house back into a home in the way that only a woman could.

How was it possible that John didn't remember?

"You sent off for a mail-order bride, John." Matt spoke quietly. "She's supposed to be arriving right after we get back from Fort Worth. The two of you are getting married... well, I suppose you're already married on account of the proxy."

A flicker of understanding lit John's eyes. His lips tilted into a smile. "Yes," he whispered.

"You've gone on and on about her."

John nodded. "I told her my brothers didn't want her to come."

Matt grimaced. It was true that Luke, Thomas and he had all tried to talk John out of bringing a stranger onto the family ranch. The woman would take up residence here, live in the old family homestead and care for the baby. Yet, who really knew anything about *her*? The only man who might have an inkling lay in bed with poison eating away at his body. Drifting in and out of confusion, John seemed to grow worse even over the course of the short conversation. Matt's heart twisted with pain. John's suffering was almost more than he could bear.

He smiled at John, hoping he looked encouraging. "I guess she's coming anyway... a pretty little blonde like Mary."

John sniffed, his eyes welled with tears. "Mary... oh, Mary, I've missed you so."

Matt suppressed a groan. "Mary's gone. And we all miss her, but you have a new wife coming. Soon."

"Mary," John whispered, staring at a spot past Matt's shoulder.

Matt wanted to suggest that John write the girl and tell her to wait. The look in John's eyes gave him a different idea. Matt didn't like the notion of a mail-order bride and had argued against it from the beginning, but now he realized the girl might eventually be useful. John was heartsick about Mary, but maybe he could gather some enthusiasm about a second chance.

"You got to do what the doc says. You've got a wife coming in a few weeks and we need you well for your new bride."

John closed his eyes. For a moment, Matt thought he'd drifted off, but then John's lids fluttered, and he opened his eyes. His expression was vacant. It was the same look John had in the months after his wife's death. Hollow.

"Doc's mentioned a couple of times that he might need to take the leg," John rasped. "How am I going to take care of a ranch and a new bride if I just got one leg? Why, I'd be no better than half a man."

Matt scrubbed a hand across his face. For the last year, he and John hadn't been close, but he still loved his brother. He respected him, too. Even though John had been reckless and impossible since Mary died, he still worked from sun-up till dusk and would go home to try and be both mama and papa to his daughter.

He owed his brother a great deal, not just because they were kin, but because John had saved his life. He wondered if John remembered that day. The man's mind was muddled from grief and pain. Maybe he'd forgotten. Matt rubbed his hand over the scars that lined the side of his face.

"You recall the day we ran into the mountain lion?"

John cracked his lids open. "Course I do."

"Lucky for me, you're a good shot. Even when you were just a boy."

"I'd never been so scared in my life."

"You and me both."

John raised his hand and gestured towards Matt's ragged scar. "Sorry I didn't get him a little sooner."

Matt shrugged. "Think how good lookin' I could have been."

John gave a weak smile. "Quit bellyaching about your scars. No one cares about them 'cept you. The right woman won't care one bit."

"If you say so. You get some rest," Matt said. "We'll talk some more when Doc comes after lunch."

John closed his eyes and sank back into the bedding. After Matt drew the drapes, he left the room and went to John's study. He needed to tell the girl about John's condition. If he sent the girl a letter, she'd get it a few days before she was to get on the train. He hated to interfere with his brother's plans but felt he had no choice. His letter would simply suggest postponing her trip, not cancelling it.

He sat down with a heavy sigh and rifled through John's letter box. What kind of girl answered a mail-ordered bride announcement? Some sort of floozy, most likely. Or a gold-digger. Either way, for now, the girl would have to stay put.

He found an envelope with her return address. For a long moment, he studied the elegant script on the front. His uncharitable thoughts of her fell to the wayside. Suddenly, he imagined a refined and delicate woman, one that would arrive to the rough town of Magnolia and be taken aback. This wasn't Boston. She might not even like it here. Then what? Would she and John annul the marriage?

One thing was certain – Matt was glad he would never take a wife. Too much trouble. At times, mostly when he was good and tired at the end of a long day, he liked the idea of coming home to a wife, and all the joys she would bring. But then the stark reality came back to him in a hurry. Texas was a hard land for women. Danger abounded everywhere, from rough men to flash floods or rattlesnakes. Not to mention the danger of childbirth. He shook his head. No, marriage was one headache he didn't need.

A soft hint of lilac wafted from the paper. A small lock of hair peeked from between the sheets of paper. Before he could stop himself, he opened the letter. The strand of hair fell to the desk.

It wasn't blonde. It was a deep, coppery red.

Matt frowned and picked up the lock of hair. All along, John had carried on about Grace, especially how she would be a pretty little blonde, just like his Mary. The memory of John's words left a hollow feeling inside Matt's chest. Grace was a redhead. John, in the depths of his grief, had turned her into a version of Mary.

That was what grief did to a man. It made him lose his mind. John was an example of just that very thing. His brother was a shattered man. A shadow of his former self. This was another reason why Matt vowed he'd never marry. He'd seen his father die of a broken heart and seen other men break after losing their wives.

Mostly he tried to avoid the fairer sex. His scar didn't earn many admiring looks. He always told himself he was too busy to chase a pretty girl. He had a ranch to run.

Marriage wasn't for him. And maybe when John got better, Matt could talk some sense into his brother. It wasn't fair to the Boston girl to come to a house with a man who was still in love with his dead wife.

Chapter Three

Grace

The train conductor was kind enough to reserve a private car just for women. Grace wasn't certain if that was customary, but after she'd seen some of the roughnecks boarding in Boston, she felt grateful for his thoughtfulness and gallantry. The young man moved along the aisle, checking on the ladies, politely offering to stow their luggage overhead.

The woman seated next to Grace told him what a fine young man he was.

He tipped his hat and gave her a broad smile. "Thank you, ma'am. Just doing things the way I'd like them done for my wife. Just got married last month."

There was a small murmur of surprise that moved through the women.

"What's her name?" Grace's companion asked.

"Her name's Lizzy." He paused to hoist a bag to the rack. "We've been childhood sweethearts."

After that there was no peace for the young man. When he passed through the car, checking tickets or on some errand, the women would talk amongst themselves, but louder than necessary, about what a lucky girl his wife was. He'd blush furiously, which only encouraged the merry group to tease him more.

Grace felt far too shy to say anything, but she enjoyed the banter. She never spoke to men if she could help it. Anytime she had to say something, she'd feel overcome with awkwardness. Painful memories of her father made her avoid men as much as possible. Of course, she'd have to talk with John. She knew that and prayed that by the time she arrived in Texas, she'd feel a glimmer of courage. She hoped he would be delighted with her early arrival.

She made herself as comfortable as possible as dusk gathered. She ate a small sandwich from the dining car. John had sent enough money for a ticket for a sleeping car, but Grace couldn't bring herself to indulge in such extravagance. Instead, she bought a first-class ticket, with a comfortable enough seat, and gave the left-over funds to her sister Faith to tuck away.

One never knew when the two girls might face an emergency. The thought made a shudder roll through her body. She squeezed her eyes shut, pushing the thought away. When she opened them again, she tried to give her attention to the lovely landscape. They were passing through thickly forested lands. The dense trees all but blocked the fading sunset to the west and made her feel as though she was traveling through a tunnel.

Towards what, she couldn't imagine. John wrote such short, terse letters. Perhaps that was the way with men. She knew he was in mourning and made a note not to tire him with too much idle chatter. She wanted to be as inconspicuous as possible. Theirs might not be a love of the ages, but she'd be certain to be agreeable and do her best. So much depended on an amiable marriage, not the least of which was a small motherless girl. Sweet Abigail. Grace yearned to care for the child and perhaps even bring some joy into her life.

After she and John and Abigail got used to each other, Grace would attempt to convince John to send for her sisters. *It would work.* She repeated the phrase in her mind, keeping time with the chug of the wheels.

Sometime in the middle of the night, Grace awakened. The train had stopped at a small town. The conductor entered the car as he spoke to a new passenger, a woman. He offered words of comfort as he ushered her into the cabin. He spoke softly. In the dim light, Grace could see that the young woman wept.

"There, there, miss. You can sleep here, and in the morning it will all be better. You'll see." He gestured to a seat across from Grace.

During the night, Grace heard snippets of the girl's story. She'd been left at the altar, jilted, and now was going to visit her sister. A wash of cold dread crept over Grace. What if John didn't want her? What if he found her ugly, or lacking in some way?

She liked to think she was pleasant looking. The three O'Brian girls often received compliments, but how could a woman really know? To make matters worse, a woman could be pleasing but less so than another woman. A thousand doubts plagued her mind. The night drifted into morning as the train continued west.

She fretted and wished she could have a basin of water to wash up. The train offered no such amenities. By the time the train arrived in Kansas City, Grace felt as though every inch of her body was covered in grit. The pretty traveling dress Faith had made for her was filthy. The hem was as dark as soot. The sleeves and cuffs were no longer a beautiful, robin's egg blue, but more of a slate gray. Her hair refused to stay pinned, traitorous curls escaping at every turn. She imagined that she looked a sight. Probably like a lost and bedraggled alley cat.

John Bentley might take one look at her and send her straight back to Boston.

Finally, the time had come. The train rolled into the Magnolia Station. Of course, there was no one to greet her. John wouldn't expect her for weeks yet. Her arrival would be a surprise, but hopefully a welcome one.

She thanked the young man who'd cared for her and her companions. Before leaving the train platform, she summoned the courage to give him a small, lace hanky. It was one of her finer pieces, a delicate French pattern with tiny roses along the border.

"Here's a little something for your Lizzy."

The young man looked bowled over. For a moment he just stared at the small offering. Then he seemed to remember his manners and swept his cap from his head. He gave a small awkward bow and grinned.

"I always try to bring her a little gift. Usually it's a book from a book shop in Santa Fe, or a candy from Fort Worth. I've never brought her something as fine as this."

Grace smiled. "Thank you for your kindness."

"Yes, miss. It was my honor. Safe travels."

A porter helped Grace with her bag, delivering it to the edge of the platform. The depot was a hive of activity, but after asking a few of the townspeople, she located a family who lived near John Bentley and agreed to take her.

The wife, a fresh-faced woman who was only a few years older than Grace, gave her a friendly smile as they set off.

"Have you traveled far?" she asked.

"All the way from Boston."

"That is a long way. I'm sure you've come to care for Abigail, the poor child."

Grace nodded. "That's my intention."

"I knew Mary, her mother. A more devoted woman you've never known. Poor Abigail is quite alone in the world now. Breaks my heart."

Grace drew a deep sigh. Somewhere between the lines of John's letters, she'd almost imagined he still pined for Mary. She tried to put it out of her mind. But meeting a woman face-to-face that knew Mary was an odd feeling. She wondered if she would be able to do as fine a job with the child as Mary would have. In her heart, she was certain she wouldn't. How could she, a veritable stranger with no experience with children, be able to perform the role of mother?

Something twisted in her heart. She winced. The pain wasn't so much to her pride, although there was that. It was more the notion that if she failed at this, she might cause irreparable harm to a poor child. A dear, sweet child that had already suffered so much loss. She said a silent prayer, yet again, that she might do a good job for the little girl.

Abigail... I'm coming. I'll do my best...

She patted the pocket inside her dress where she carried the marriage proxy, assuring herself that it was still there. The paper crinkled under her palm. John had sent two copies. Her instructions were to sign both, keep one and send the other back. She'd done as directed, and that meant that somewhere in the Bentley household was a copy of the proxy with her signature.

The wagon bumped along the road. Grace admired the wide-open spaces and enormous oak trees. Cattle grazed in the verdant meadows. Barns dotted the hillside.

"Texas is lovely, isn't it?" she murmured.

Her companion beamed. “We all think so. It’s home. You know?”

Grace willed her shoulders to relax and sink a little. “Yes,” she said. “It is home.”

“Where will you take Abigail?”

“Pardon me?”

The woman knit her brow. “Surely you won’t stay in the house by yourself. It wouldn’t be safe. A woman alone.”

Grace was taken aback. Why did the woman regard her with such sympathy? Surely there was nothing wrong with the Bentley home. And why would she suggest it wasn’t safe? Her heart raced, hammering against her ribs.

“I’ve come to care for Abigail,” she said carefully, feeling painfully awkward with the words she uttered, “because I am here to care for her as her new mother. I’m here to wed John Bentley. In fact, I’m already his wife by proxy.”

The woman drew a sharp breath. The words hung in the air, making Grace’s skin prickle with discomfort. She watched with growing dismay as the woman paled.

Her companion’s hand fluttered to her throat. “Oh.” She bit her lip and blinked several times. “Oh, dear.”

Chapter Four

Matt

The days leading up to the cattle drive were hectic as usual. The cowboys had rounded up over a thousand yearlings, and the animals stood in the pens, jostling each other and bawling. They wanted out. They wanted their mamas and they wanted to kick up their heels like any youngster.

Usually, Matt looked forward to a cattle drive. This time around, as the time to depart drew closer, he realized he wouldn't be making the trip with John. The idea of going without his brother disheartened him.

The Bentley brothers owned plots of land on the family ranch, probably because they quarreled and argued endlessly. Each brother thought the others were obstinate and impossible. The twice-yearly trips to Fort Worth united them with a single purpose. They always traveled together. And when they stayed in the big city, they ate supper together each evening, enjoying each other's company while they debated just about everything under the sun.

This year, John wasn't going. It was clear. Matt hadn't realized how bad the leg was until a day after he'd seen the nurse change the dressing. He went to visit John and found him sleeping. He tried to wake him but failed.

The nurse and doctor arrived a few minutes later, their expressions ashen. It was then that Matt realized John would never go on another cattle drive. Ever.

By morning John had succumbed.

Matt and his brothers buried him beside their parents and Mary. The pastor came from two towns over. A small service was held. All the while, Abigail wept pitifully. Matt tried to console her, as did Luke and Thomas, but to no avail. Finally, the child's nursemaid, Bernice, bundled her off to the nursery, frowning and grumbling all the way.

Matt brought the nursemaid and the child to his home, so the girl would be near family instead of residing in John's empty house with no company other than an irritable nursemaid. Matt left his cook, Harriet, in charge of the household.

Determined to make the trip to Fort Worth, the three brothers departed at dawn the day after John's funeral. Matt told them about the letter to John's mail-order bride, and that he'd sent a second one via express mail after John died.

"Seems a pity," Luke said over dinner their first night in Fort Worth. "If she came she might be a comfort to Abigail."

Matt scoffed. "A woman she's never laid eyes on. Doubtful."

"John saw something in the girl. Surely she's a good woman."

"We'll never know now." Matt pushed his plate aside. He had no appetite in the days since John passed. "Once she gets the letter, I'm sure that will be the end of it. Most likely won't hear another word from the girl."

Thomas spoke wearily. "We need to find a better nursemaid for Abigail. Bernice is about as kind and loving as a saddle-sore mule."

"One thing at a time," Matt said.

"One of us needs to take the child in," Thomas said. "I already have my hands full. I've got ranch duties and sheriff duties. Not to mention a boy to raise."

Matt grimaced. Thomas was right. He did have his hands full, raising a boy he claimed as his own, even though everyone knew the boy wasn't his. His brother had been duped into marriage and left a widower when his wife passed away.

On top of that he was pressed into duty as the town sheriff and that took him into town several days a week.

Luke, the youngest of the Bentley brothers, was too bent on enjoying life and holding off marriage for as long as possible. Luke couldn't possibly take care of a child. At any given moment, he'd likely forget about her entirely and head into town to play cards.

"Looks like the girl will be with me for the time being," Matt said. "It's fine. She's not much trouble. Mostly I feel sorry for her. Terrible to lose both parents so young."

"What's going to happen to John's house?" Thomas asked.

Matt shrugged. "I don't know."

"Maybe I'll take the house," Thomas muttered. "And find a wife to teach my son some manners."

Instead of staying in Fort Worth for several days, Matt resolved to return to Magnolia. His brothers tried to convince him to stay. There'd be a few dinners they could attend and all the ranchers' pretty daughters to flirt with, but Matt had no use for ranchers' daughters. The parties held after the auction always left him feeling restless and uncomfortable. The pretty daughters often looked upon him with a mix of alarm and pity. His scars seemed to draw their attention in a way that made social events nothing more than a trial.

He turned for home as soon as the cattle sales were complete. He bid his brothers good-bye and started the long ride alone. The trip went slowly. First, his horse threw a shoe, forcing him to stay overnight in a small town just outside of Fort Worth. Then the weather turned bad. It rained day and night. Twice he had to take a detour to find a passable bridge.

When he arrived in Magnolia, he went directly to the post office which also served as the town's telegraph office.

The clerk came to the window. Roy was elderly and kindly and had been the postmaster ever since Matt could remember. They exchanged pleasantries for a moment before Roy's expression grew solemn.

"Alice and I were sorry to hear about John's passing. Such a tragedy."

Matt nodded. "John wasn't ever the same after Mary died."

"To think that little girl's left with neither mama nor daddy. Just three bachelor uncles to raise her."

"We got a nursemaid to take care of day-to-day things, but it's not the same."

Roy nodded. "Bernice's all right, I suppose. I knew her growing up and she was always the meanest kid on the playground."

Matt was taken aback. "That so? I'd never heard that. Wonder why John hired her on?"

"Probably not thinking clearly after he lost Mary."

An unease crept into Matt's thoughts. He recalled the hard expression on Bernice's face when Abigail cried. The woman had never married and never raised her own children. What could she know about little ones?

"I'd best get back," he said. "You have any letters for me? I'm expecting a letter or telegraph from Boston."

Roy went to the letter boxes and rifled through a stack of letters and telegraph messages. "I don't believe I have anything for you, Matt."

"Thank you. Say, if you know of anyone who could tend to John's daughter, would you give me a shout? I might just start fresh with a new nursemaid. I'd like someone mature, like Bernice, but a little softer spoken. It would be best to avoid hiring on a young lady with me being a bachelor, if you get my meaning."

"I thought I heard you had a new girl out there. I could have sworn I saw a pretty redhead carrying Abigail the other day in the mercantile."

Matt shook his head. "I don't have a new girl. Not yet. But soon, maybe."

Roy nodded. "I'll talk to Alice. We'll help in any way we can."

"Much obliged." Matt turned out of the post office and mounted his horse. He was anxious to look in on little Abigail. Almost as anxious as he was to soak in a hot bath and put on some dry clothes.

He turned his gelding toward home and set off at a lope.

Chapter Five

Grace

The news of John's death shocked Grace beyond words. Unsure what to do next, she decided the best course of action was to see to the baby. She was told that Abigail stayed with one of John's brothers. The couple who she'd met at the station offered to take her. As she drew near the farmhouse, she wavered in her decision. Was it her duty? What would John want her to do?

Most importantly, what was *right*?

The couple who brought her had done so out of Christian duty. Grace could see that clearly. Once they'd let her off they seemed overly eager to be on their way. Grace could hardly blame them. Part of her wanted to run after the wagon and beg them to take her, anywhere really.

She stood at the bottom of the porch steps, her heart pounding. Dogs trotted up to her, barked a few times and then ambled to a nearby tree. They flopped on the ground but watched her with interest.

The house was much finer than she expected. A two-story clapboard farmhouse. Painted a light blue with white shutters, it looked cheerful and inviting despite the circumstances.

A woman stepped out, dragging a rolled-up rug. When she saw Abigail, she dropped the rug and yelped with surprise. "Who are you?"

Grace swallowed, trying to dislodge the lump in her throat.

"My name is Grace O'Brian."

"I'm Harriet Patchwell. The cook. Is Mr. Bentley expecting you?"

"I doubt it. I'm John Bentley's mail-ordered bride. I've just arrived from Boston."

The woman stared, slack-jawed. Slowly her expression shifted to wry amusement. Her lips curved into a smile. "You've come for Abigail."

"I felt I should check in on her. I understand John has passed, but I wanted to make certain the child is in good hands."

The woman bobbed her head. "Thank the good Lord. His nursemaid is a tyrant."

Grace recoiled. "A tyrant?"

"Oooh, I wouldn't wish that nursemaid on any child."

Grace wondered what Mrs. Patchwell meant. Worry knotted inside her. Either way, she'd have to speak to Abigail's uncle even though she had no authority whatsoever.

"Is Mr. Matthew Bentley at home?"

"He's gone to Fort Worth."

A huff of surprise fell from Grace's lips. "He left the baby with the..."

The woman nodded. "The tyrant."

"When will he return?"

"He didn't say."

"Dear heavens. I should see to the child." Grace bent to pick up her bag, but the woman waved her hand.

"Let me send someone to take your bag, Mrs. Bentley."

"But I'm not-"

"Please. I won't hear of you carrying your own bag, Mrs. Bentley. You have a baby who needs looking in on."

The woman stepped over the rug, went to the front door and held it open.

Grace ascended the steps and paused in the doorway. She gave the woman an awkward smile. "This seems like some sort of terrible dream."

The woman sighed. "Imagine how the little girl feels. She's missing both her mother and father."

"Of course," Grace said hastily. "My troubles are nothing compared to that."

She stepped inside the house and stopped to take in the interior. Feeling grubby and disheveled, she noted the lovely furnishings and fine rugs. The wood floor, polished to a fine sheen, reflected the light that streamed in through the windows.

"Is there a Mrs. Bentley?" Grace asked.

Mrs. Patchwell snorted. "There isn't. The Bentley men are too ornery."

Before Grace could reply, a small cry came from upstairs. The plaintive sound was followed by a strident voice.

"You're not done with your nap, you little brat. Hush now, before I give you a reason to cry."

Without waiting another moment, Grace crossed the parlor, hurried down the hall and up the stairs as quickly as she could. She rushed down the hallway to the end where she found the nursery. A woman stood over the crib, shouting and waving her arms about. Grace was certain the woman intended to strike the child. With a cry of anger, Grace dashed across the room and stepped in front of the woman.

The woman's face twisted with fury. It was clear the nursemaid was in fighting spirits. She narrowed her beady eyes and pressed her lips into a sneer. "Who do you think you are?"

"I am Abigail's mother." Her words were followed by a small huff of surprise. Her own surprise. The words had spilled, unbidden from her lips, tumbling out on a wave of anger she'd never known.

The woman paled and recoiled. After she stumbled back several steps, Grace tore her gaze from her and turned to the child, cowering in the crib. The little girl huddled in the furthest corner of the crib. Tears streaked her face. Her chin trembled. Small tendrils of flaxen hair clung to her flushed skin.

Grace's heart lurched in her chest. For months she'd tried to picture the child. Every mile of her journey to Texas, she imagined a small, motherless waif. Never did she consider she might find the child trembling in her own bed, the very picture of heartbreak.

Grace held out her arms, beckoning the small girl. "Come, Abigail. I've got you now."

The small girl whimpered. Her gaze drifted to the nursemaid and back to Grace. She seemed to be weighing her options. The child wore a stained gown. Filth caked her sleeves and her face was unwashed.

"Come, darling," Grace whispered on a prayer.

The girl crept across the crib and slowly pulled herself up. She gazed at Grace, tears glistening on her lashes. When Grace lifted her, she held her against her chest and wrapped her arms around the child's trembling body. It took a moment for Grace to realize the baby's dress was wet. Soaked, really.

"When was the last time this child had a dry diaper?" she asked, barely able to contain her anger.

The nursemaid lifted her chin. "I don't answer to you."

Grace pursed her lips and moved to the changing table by the window. Gently, she lay the child down, and, keeping a hand on her so she wouldn't roll away, Grace tugged the marriage proxy from her dress pocket. She held it up for the woman's inspection.

"I am Mrs. John Bentley. And you are dismissed. You will pack your things and leave this house at once."

Chapter Six

Matt

Augustus stood in the barnyard when Matt rode up. The old foreman grinned at him and waved. The friendly greeting was a little unexpected on account of the way things had been between them when Matt left for Fort Worth. He'd asked Gus to stay at the ranch. Normally, Gus would have ridden with the other cowboys. He had more experience than any of the others, but Matt wanted someone to remain behind.

If the child needed something, Gus would be available to hitch the wagon and take Bernice to town. Gus could fetch the doctor if the baby took ill. There were a number of reasons the old-timer needed to stay back. He'd grumbled plenty when Matt told him the news, but now he was all smiles.

The dogs bounded into the farmyard, barking and wagging their tails. Matt dismounted and bent down to scratch them behind their ears. The dogs panted and tussled, happy he was home. Matt had to admit it *was* good to be home.

"You're back early," Gus said.

Matt handed off his reins. "I wanted to make sure the baby was settled. I didn't feel right riding off and leaving Abigail. Poor little thing."

"The last few days she's been all smiles when I seen her."

Matt took off his hat and wiped his brow. His hat still dripped water drops from the constant rain he'd endured. "Abigail smiling? You don't say."

"She's a sweet little mite, especially when she laughs. She seems to have taken a fancy to butterflies. Tries to catch them."

Matt smiled at the thought of his brother's child finding some small shred of happiness. At less than a year, she'd lost both parents. She'd been despondent after her mother's death. He expected that after John died, she would slip further into melancholy. Matt found the child bewildering. If John had left a son behind, perhaps it would have been a little easier. Even John had seemed at a loss when it came to his daughter. He avoided her. Probably because she reminded him of Mary.

"Warms my heart to hear it, Gus. I thank you for staying behind. Next time I'll be sure to-"

The sound of a child's laughter floated on the late evening breeze. Matt scanned the rose garden, seeking the source of the joyful noise. Little Abigail emerged from behind a rose bush. She ran, awkwardly, arms outstretched towards a butterfly. Her blonde curls shone in the sunshine. Her face was bathed in golden light. Matt couldn't help but laugh to see the happy little girl.

She tripped and tumbled to the grass. Her spill made her laugh all the more. A moment later a woman appeared from behind the roses. She ran to Abigail, leaned down and swept her into her arms. The woman's laughter mingled with the child's as she twirled. Abigail shrieked with delight and the woman drew her in for a tender embrace. The pair strolled down the path to the back of the house. Abigail babbled happily as she sat on the woman's hip. A moment later the two disappeared into the house. Matt stared, slack-jawed, wondering why his mind was playing tricks on him.

"Gus?"

"Yes, sir."

"I don't recall Bernice having red hair."

Gus knit his brow. "Bernice had gray hair. You get too much sun?"

Matt studied the back door of the house, trying to sort out if he imagined things. "I didn't get too much sun. It rained the entire time. Cats and dogs."

Gus pointed a gnarled finger towards the house. "That ain't Bernice."

"I see that."

Matt waited for Gus to say more, and the man clearly waited for the same thing.

"That red-haired lady is Mrs. Bentley," Gus said. "John's widow. Remember he sent for a bride? I thought you knew."

"Mrs... Bentley?"

"She don't like to be called that, since she and John didn't exchange vows. She says she don't have a right to the name. Everyone calls her Miss O'Brian."

"Miss O'Brian."

"Uh-huh."

Suddenly Matt felt bone-tired. He wanted nothing more than to get out of his wet boots and enjoy a nice dinner in his home. Preferably alone. Now he had a woman to contend with. "When did she get here?"

"The day you left for Fort Worth."

"I see." He didn't really, but what more could he say?

"First thing she did is run off Bernice."

"What?"

Gus grinned. "Sent her packing. That old biddy was too mean to be a nursemaid. I'd say it wasn't a moment too soon. Harriet was plotting to get rid of her. Somehow. She wouldn't tell me what she had planned, but Harriet was madder than a wet hen about the way Bernice treated the child. I'd say Miss O'Brian prolly kept Harriet from some sort of deadly deed."

Matt curled his hands into fists. "You mean to tell me that you let a complete stranger into my home, to care for my niece?"

Gus shrugged. "She ain't a *complete* stranger. She's John's widow."

Matt dragged his fingers through his hair. "She isn't John's widow, either. They never married."

"She's got a marriage proxy, signed by John. Saw it myself. She showed it to me and Harriet. Course, Harriet didn't care who she was. We were all just mighty glad she got rid of Bernice the grouch."

Matt suppressed a groan. If Harriet liked the girl there might be no getting rid of her. Harriet might only be the cook, but she ruled over the house like a mostly benevolent duchess, or queen maybe.

"And then she gave Harriet a lace shawl, one she made herself, and there was no going back after that. Harriet thinks she's hung the moon. You can't believe the way she goes on about the lace and what a fine lady Miss O'Brian is."

"I can hear it now," Matt said wearily. He turned towards the house, leaving his foreman without another word. His boots made squelching noises as he walked. He gritted his teeth, trying to imagine what he would tell the girl. Get out of my house? Go back to Boston? Never come back?

He snorted. Maybe all three. He paused at the door for a long moment. If he stormed inside, he might frighten her.

Worse, he might frighten Abigail. She was such a delicate little thing and he'd made her dissolve in tears once when he spoke too loudly, fussing at the dogs.

Drawing a deep breath, he pulled the door open gently, shutting it behind himself. He walked upstairs, down the hallway to the nursery. The woman's humming filled the silence. Matt paused at the doorway. He wanted to go in, but somehow felt as though he was intruding. The notion only made him more exasperated. He felt like a stranger in this part of the house. The nursery.

He shook off the thought and nudged the door open. The woman held the baby, who nestled against her, melting into her arms. The sight of her, in the last rays of dusk, humming softly, made his thoughts scatter. Suddenly, he couldn't remember the girl's name. It was ridiculous, he told himself. He'd written her a letter and addressed the envelope. The memory came back to him.

Grace O'Brian...

He recalled the tiny lock of hair she'd sent John. Her hair hung down her back and swayed softly as she rocked the baby from side to side. He waited and watched as she moved slowly to the crib. Gently, she lowered the sleeping child to the bed. She leaned over and arranged the blankets around the girl.

Matt retreated several steps. It wouldn't do to stand in the doorway and startle her or the baby. From the hallway, he listened a moment longer. Her voice was soft, lilting, the tone comforting him somehow. He wanted to linger. Instead, he returned downstairs and waited for Grace.

Chapter Seven

Grace

With Abigail down for the evening, Grace went downstairs, straight to the kitchen and found her dinner warming in the oven. Since Mr. Bentley wasn't expected home for several more days, Harriet had gone to her sister's that afternoon. The notion that Grace had the house to herself unsettled her. She'd been here for over a week, but this would be the first night alone.

She pushed her unease aside. Caring for Abigail wore her out. She might feel some prickling worry now, as the dusk gave way to night, but once in bed, she'd sleep soundly. Since coming to Magnolia, she hadn't had a single nightmare.

The waning light cast shadows across the kitchen. Grace moved to the lamp, thinking to light it. She struck the match but paused. Footfalls echoed in the house. They drew closer. Heavy, purposeful, they were not the footsteps of Harriet, but of someone larger. A man. She knew without a doubt. With a quick puff, she blew out the match. Looking around the kitchen desperately, she spied a rolling pin and grabbed it off the counter.

Perhaps it was Gus or another ranch hand, but to be safe, she wanted something in her hand. Harriet had made a few vague references to the Sanders family. They were dangerous men who might try to cause her trouble if given half a chance.

The thought of Abigail drove her to do things she'd never considered, like grabbing a kitchen tool that could serve as a weapon.

The footsteps came to a halt at the door. A soft rap sounded. She waited, slowly lifting the rolling pin should the man burst into the kitchen and try to do her harm.

Abigail was upstairs. Dear God. How would she protect the baby against an intruder? Her breath grew shallow. Her heart thudded. “Come in.”

The door pushed open. A man stepped forward, filling the doorframe. He frowned at the upraised rolling pin but didn't seem terribly concerned.

“Evening, Miss O'Brian. I'm Matt Bentley. John's brother.”

In the dim light, it was impossible to make out his expression, but she was sure she heard a wry smile in his voice. He waited for her to respond. She couldn't. Her words lodged in her throat.

“You can put the rolling pin down.” He took a step forward. “Unless you intend to make a pie.”

She lowered the rolling pin but did not set it aside. Not yet. She bit her lip, wondering how to proceed. This was awkward. Far beyond awkward. She knew this day was coming, the day she'd come face to face with Abigail's uncle, but she'd assumed she still had time to prepare.

He took off his hat and set it aside. He moved to the sideboard, struck a match and after it sparked and flared, he lit the lamp. Shadows danced along the walls. He glanced at the rolling pin, studied her for a long moment and then ambled across the room. He sat down on the far side of the table.

His steady gaze on her made it difficult to draw a proper breath. The entire scene played out like a very bad dream. She stood in a stranger's home and threatened him with a rolling pin, not that it was much of a threat, considering his immense height and powerful build.

"I didn't expect you," she stammered, setting the rolling pin aside.

He drummed his fingers on the table, mulling over her words. "*You* didn't expect *me*?"

It was clear he thought her words were ridiculous. She could hardly deny they sounded absurd, but resented the mocking tone of his voice. He tilted his head to one side, studying her as if she were some sort of oddity.

"I didn't expect you. No. They said you'd stay in Fort Worth a few more days yet."

He pressed his lips together and his features took on a slightly menacing expression. She wondered, briefly, if she should pick up the rolling pin once again, just in case he gave a show of anger. She glanced at it, giving herself away. He sighed heavily.

"You can't stay here," he said.

"No, of course not."

For a moment he didn't speak. Finally, he smiled. "That was easier than I imagined."

"Well, Mr. Bentley, it's hardly proper. I can't stay in a home with a man who is not my husband."

"Right."

"In the morning, I'll collect Abigail and take her back to John's house. Er... Abigail's house." She gave a nervous laugh. "I mean my and Abigail's house."

He leaned forward, resting his weight on his elbows. "You have to go back to Boston."

Any trace of humor vanished from his eyes. His mouth thinned to a grim expression. He was a man who got his way.

A man who issued orders. A man not used to explaining himself, certainly not to a stranger, a woman at that.

The last thing she wanted to do was argue with a man in his own house. But she was determined to remain in Magnolia. The memory of Abigail, wide-eyed and cowering in her bed, gave her a small surge of bravery. She took a deep, trembling breath. "I will not. I'm devoted to Abigail."

"So am I."

"If you were, why did you leave her with that horrible woman?"

"I had no choice."

His dismissive tone emboldened her. "You don't have a choice now, either." She gulped, half-expecting him to fly into a rage at her words. Instead he regarded her with disbelief. She forged on. "Legally, I am Abigail's mother and guardian. I have the proxy to prove it."

Her heart crashed against her ribs. Dear God, she'd just told off a man, something she'd never done once in her life. She'd always backed away from any sort of confrontation, preferring to avoid strife. She wasn't the brave one, not like Faith. But faced with being torn from Abigail, she felt as fierce as a mother lion. Abigail, poor, dear Abigail, needed her to be brave, and that thought inspired her like nothing before.

He shook his head but remained silent.

"What difference is it to you?" she asked. "John left behind a little money, I assume, and a house. I'll make use of it and care for the girl. She..." Her words faltered. A wave of emotion came over her and when she continued her voice shook. "She needs me."

It was true. She felt it deep in her heart. The first few days she'd spent with Abigail, the child's eyes held a sadness that wrenched Grace's heart. After several days, something changed. The child started smiling. Her silence gave way to babbling. Her smiles turned to laughter. Grace had marveled at the transformation. Harriet had called it a small miracle.

Grace wasn't one to boast, but she liked to think that she'd brought the change about. Abigail *did* need her. And she needed Abigail.

Mr. Bentley scowled at her. "John had little money. Much of anything lately, 'cept bad luck. It was my money that brought you here."

She straightened and gave him a prim look. His assertion shocked her. The notion that Mr. Bentley paid her way to Texas left her on uncertain ground. Perhaps he was trying to get the upper hand. Did John leave debts? Now was hardly the time to discuss accounts and balances. Whatever hardship lay before didn't concern her as much as Abigail's well-being.

"No matter. I need little. The child probably doesn't have many needs at this point of her young life. I'll stay in the house, care for her. And at a later date, I intend to send for my sisters."

He shook his head. "No. No sisters."

"I beg your pardon?"

His gaze darkened. "No. Sisters."

Swallowing hard, she waited for him to clarify this mandate. It was none of his concern. She wondered frantically why he was so set against her bringing her family to Texas. Why would a man like him have any opinion one way or another?

"A single, young woman will attract plenty of attention. Our family has dangerous enemies. It would be worse if there are three women living out there alone. Without a man around."

"The three of us lived alone in Boston."

"Not the same."

"I don't have to answer to you, Mr. Bentley." Her heart thundered in her chest, but she forged on regardless. "I am John's widow. Legally."

She could sense a slow anger building in him. He'd like to throw her out. If he did that tonight, she'd be powerless to stop him. She'd be cast out and would have little recourse other than to sleep on the porch swing. Or perhaps she could find shelter with Mr. Bentley's cook. Harriet seemed to have a soft spot in her heart for her.

Surely he wouldn't send her from the house. Gus had told her that the Bentley men were the finest around. Honest. Hard-working. God-fearing.

"John's legal widow. His land, that's what's on your mind. You're a rich widow now, aren't you? Did you go visit the bank first thing?"

Grace's mouth opened but her words of protest died in her throat. She sank into the chair. He thought she was nothing more than a money-grubber. How could she argue that? She had no proof otherwise.

"You presume, Mr. Bentley," she finally managed.

"Do I? Have you been to town?"

"I have. I went to the mercantile to buy wool, so I could make Abigail a few hats. It's often cool in the evenings and I didn't want her to catch a chill."

He rubbed his jaw, mulling over her words. "Did you charge it to the Bentley account?"

She drew a trembling breath, trying to tamp down her indignation. "I've never charged anything in my life. The O'Brian Family subscribes to the belief of neither a borrower nor a lender be. I paid with my own coin."

"That so?"

"You don't believe me?"

He gave her an appraising look. "No. I reckon I do believe you."

"How generous."

Her words drew a chuckle from him. His amusement sparked her ire. She pursed her lips, refusing to dignify his mirth with a response. Gus was wrong about the Bentley men, or at least he was wrong about this one. Matthew Bentley was an impossible, arrogant man who enjoyed baiting and bullying defenseless women. His uncharitable response to her reaffirmed her decision to stand by Abigail come what may.

"All right, Grace," he said, getting to his feet. "We'll let this go till morning. For tonight, I'll sleep in the bunkhouse. Thataway you'll have the house to yourself."

She wondered what letting it go till morning meant exactly. But she also heard the weariness in his voice. He, at least, showed a hint of decency by offering to sleep in the bunkhouse. She'd seen the building when she'd taken Abigail for walks. From the looks of things, it couldn't be comfortable.

Tomorrow, she'd arrange to move to John's house. She knew nothing of the home but imagined it would be comparable to Matt's. It didn't matter. If it had a roof and four walls, she'd make do. She never needed much before to be comfortable, and now was no different.

Matt got to his feet. The chair scraped the floor as he rose. He studied her for a moment or more. What did he see in her? Did he see an upstart? A nuisance?

"You're fond of the girl," he said quietly.

His words were entirely unexpected, and the tone surprised her as much as what he said. It was gentle and tender, even. Suddenly her eyes prickled with tears. Her throat felt tight and her thoughts spun as she tried to think of what to say. Was she fond of the girl? No. Her feeling ran much deeper. She'd thought of the girl day in and day out from the first moment John told her he had a daughter. From the beginning she'd felt a fierce desire to protect and love Abigail. Now that she had cared for the girl for a week, thoughts of Abigail consumed her mind from the moment she woke to the moment she collapsed in bed.

"Yes, Mr. Bentley," she whispered. "Very fond."

"I want what's best for the girl. I loved my brother, and Mary was like a sister to me. I don't know much about children though. Sometimes I think I frighten them."

He rubbed his hand over his jaw and grimaced. As he turned, she caught sight of a scar that ran down the side of his face and along his neck. She sat, holding her breath, too shocked to say a word.

"I think I frighten some women too," he said with a humorless laugh. "I've had the scar since I was a boy, when I got on the wrong side of a cougar. Sometimes I forget it's there."

"My word..." Her words trailed off.

"A case of bad luck." His voice was bitter.

"On the contrary. I'd say it was a tremendous amount of good luck. He came close to your eye."

He gave her a puzzled look. Silence stretched between them. Grace couldn't recall a more unusual conversation. A moment ago, he demanded that she return to Boston, and now he spoke casually of a grave childhood injury. She had the impression he didn't speak of this often, perhaps ever. Why would he share the story with her?

After an awkward moment, he spoke. "I'll need to get a change of clothes, but then I'll head down to the bunkhouse. If you need something, anything, you know where to find me."

"Thank you."

"I should just offer for you," he said gruffly.

She took a step back. Her hand fluttered to her throat. Offer for her? She'd scarcely gotten accustomed to the idea of being a widow. This man wanted to offer for her? The notion bewildered her. "Mr. Bentley, I don't even know you."

He seemed not to notice her comments. In the shadowed light she saw him frown as he mulled over the notion. What madness. To offer marriage!

"It would be one solution to the problem."

"What problem?" she asked.

He scoffed as if she were some sort of simpleton. "The problem of you and Abigail."

"Neither of us are a problem, Mr. Bentley." She hoped her tone sounded resolute. "You needn't bother yourself with trying to find a solution."

"Never imagined getting married," he muttered darkly.

She wanted to tell him she hadn't either, that she'd entered into an arrangement with John so she could forge a path for her sisters. At least that had been her idea in the beginning. Over time she'd grown attached to his short letters. He wasn't particularly loving, or romantic, but he was so clearly in pain. She longed to come to Texas and make a home for him and his child. The words hovered in her thoughts, but she couldn't find the will to utter them aloud.

Mr. Bentley moved to the door, mumbled a good night and left the kitchen.

She sat in the darkened kitchen, her mind fraught with worry. Mr. Bentley didn't care for her at all. Well, she didn't care for him either. Not one bit. Would he make a point of making her life difficult? Was there a way to arrive at some sort of compromise? His footsteps faded as he ascended the stairs. She listened, waiting, and a short time later, he came back downstairs. The front door opened and closed, leaving the house seeped in a sudden chill and a heavy, foreboding silence.

Chapter Eight

Matt

After a restless night, Matt woke, his shoulders aching from the lumpy mattress. He grimaced as he rolled out of bed. After several nights camping along the trail to Fort Worth, and a couple of nights in hotels, he'd looked forward to his own bed. Wouldn't his brothers laugh at his ways, probably calling him an old-timer for wanting the familiarity of his bed.

He poured water into a basin, washed his face and got dressed.

The worst part of sleeping in the bunkhouse was he suspected he'd be sleeping there a while yet. Miss O'Brian wasn't going to be parted from Abigail, at least not soon. The bunkhouse was empty since his cowboys had stayed in Fort Worth for a few days as was their custom at the end of a cattle drive. In a few days they'd return, and he'd have to share the space with others. The notion held little appeal. He trudged up to the house, wincing at the crick in his neck.

As he approached the house, he realized the worst part of this wasn't bunking with the cowboys, but having a pretty woman living in his home. He imagined her moving amidst the rooms. At night she'd sleep in one of the beds upstairs. Which one, he wondered. And then his mind went to imagining what she'd look like asleep, her beautiful, red hair cast about her.

He growled and forced his thoughts back to the business at hand and went inside the house.

Harriet worked at the stove, scrambling an enormous pan of eggs. The aroma of coffee and bacon wafted through the air and made his stomach rumble. When she heard the door, she whirled around and gave him a broad smile.

“Mr. Bentley, you’re back early. I didn’t hear the dogs bark.”

“I got back last night.”

“Oh. I see.” Harriet pursed her lips and frowned at him. “Last night...”

“That’s right.”

“So you’ve met Grace?”

“I did meet Grace. I slept in the bunkhouse.”

She waved her hands. “It’s not for me to say anything about that, sir.”

Despite her words, Harriet looked very pleased. It took him all of two seconds to see the lay of the land. Clearly Harriet *and* Gus were both devoted to Grace. He grumbled under his breath as he crossed the kitchen to the stove and poured himself a cup of coffee.

Years ago, when his parents built him a house, his mother had hired Harriet to cook for him. This came after he’d sworn he’d remain a bachelor all his life. His mother fretted that he’d starve half to death and insisted he take on a cook. Harriet Patchwell was as much a fixture in his house as Gus was a permanent presence in the barnyard. Some workers came to the Bentley Brothers Ranch and stayed a season, some stayed forever.

Gus and Harriet were the forever-type. Which was a blessing, but it also meant they were more than simple workers. They had to be treated with the utmost respect.

Indulged. Especially the cook. It was never a good idea to make the cook mad. He'd found that out in a hurry back when Harriet first hired on and he'd had the bad idea of criticizing the coffee.

He shuddered at the memory. Harriet Patchwell didn't bother getting mad. She went straight for revenge. For a solid month, Harriet made nothing more than a thin porridge for breakfast. It was runny, and bad tasting. The coffee, on the other hand was so thick he practically had to chew his way through a cup. To redeem himself, Matt had to buy Harriet a new set of cooking pots for her. And her sister.

He hadn't made the same mistake again.

"I'm sure Miss Grace is a bit of a surprise." Harriet's smile lit her face with an expression of joy he'd rarely seen first thing in the morning. Usually she spent mornings glowering at everyone. Her bad mood would wear off as the day went on. By noon she might stop grousing, but never before.

"A surprise? You could say that again."

"But she's been such a blessing. I was fixing to have words with the nursemaid. Turns out, Grace saved me the trouble. And since then, Abigail, the poor little waif, has had nothing but smiles for all of us. Mostly Grace, of course."

Matt sighed and took a swallow of his coffee. "Of course."

Footsteps echoed in the upstairs hallway, then down the steps, and a moment later Grace appeared in the kitchen with Abigail on her hip. Last night, he'd spoken to Grace in this very room, but it had been lit only by candlelight. In the morning sunlight he saw her clearly. He gazed now, his cup halfway to his mouth.

Grace was younger than he'd realized. And even more beautiful. Her hair tumbled past her shoulders, soft copper curls that swayed and bounced with each step. Her skin was fair. Blue eyes, the color of summer. They widened when she saw him. Her steps faltered, and she came to a standstill. For a moment, they stared at each other.

Harriet snickered, breaking the silence. Abigail followed with a chortling sound. While Harriet's mocking laughter was nothing new, he'd rarely heard Abigail make a peep. Apart from last night when she'd chased butterflies in the garden, he rarely heard her laughing. Yet there it was, plain as day. The little girl's eyes sparkled with happiness, and something in the way she seemed to almost glow, brought a smile to his lips.

"You forget about your coffee?" Harriet asked, amusement edging her tone.

Matt realized he still stood with his coffee halfway to his mouth. He set his cup down and nodded politely at Grace. "Abigail is looking well."

His voice was a little gruffer than he intended. Despite that, Grace gave him a smile. It was slight, but it was a smile nonetheless.

"Thank you, Mr. Bentley," she replied.

She turned away, circled the kitchen table and set the child in the high chair. Matt frowned. He'd never noticed the high chair before, not here or in John's kitchen.

"Where did that come from?" he demanded.

"Gus made it for me," she replied.

She lifted her chin, as if daring him to fuss about it. Irritation simmered inside him. He tried not to watch her gather breakfast for the baby, or notice her graceful movements, but it was difficult to tear his eyes from her. She moved about the kitchen as if she had lived there for years, not days.

Casting him a wary glance, she spoke. "Could I trouble Gus to take me and Abigail home?"

"You are home," he replied, again with a gruff tone.

Harriet gave him a look of surprise. He thought he saw disapproval there too. She said nothing and turned back to making breakfast.

Grace looked flustered and a slow blush crept across her skin. "I meant John's home. I can't stay here and put you out of your own house."

"You can't live out there by yourself." Matt took a swallow of his coffee. From the corner of his eye, he noticed Harriet bobbing her head. At least they agreed on one thing. It wasn't fitting for a young woman to live alone. There had been a time when John had a cook and cowboys, ranch hands and the like, but since Mary passed away, he'd either run them off or they left on their own accord. The ranch and the house sat empty now. Even the barn cats had left.

"That's right, Grace," Harriet brought plates to the table, first serving Grace and Abigail and then Matt.

"I can't stay here," Grace said softly, offering Abigail a forkful of fluffy eggs.

"Truer words were never spoken." Matt sat down and pulled his plate closer. He ignored the daggers he assumed Harriet shot his direction.

"It's nice that we see eye-to-eye, Mr. Bentley." She took a dainty bite of the edge of her toast.

"How about I take you there and show you John's ranch?"

"Don't you mean *my* ranch?"

Matt glanced at Harriet and watched her face redden. Grace was doing a fair job trying to keep the upper hand. He'd give her that, and Harriet was trying to keep from laughing at his dilemma.

When she'd recovered, Harriet offered to make them a picnic to take along. "The little one will need a bite to eat, won't she?"

"She's eating breakfast now," Matt grumbled.

"Ooh, but they're like little birds, Mr. Bentley." Harriet drew close to Abigail and trailed her fingers through her blonde tresses. "Such a lovely little birdie, aren't you?"

Abigail smiled and kicked her feet.

"When would you like to go?" Grace asked.

"Soon as you're ready," Matt replied.

"I just need to pack my things."

"I'm just showing you around the place, that's all. Take what you need for the day. If you'll excuse me, ladies. I need to hitch the wagon."

He pushed his plate aside, took his hat from the bench and left the kitchen. He heard the women's conversation mixed with Abigail's laughter as he left the house. How had this happened? One day he was a contented bachelor. The next day he was the guardian of his niece. Today he was saddled with the child's... what? Mother? No, that wasn't right, but she wasn't a nursemaid, either.

He scowled as he made his way to the barn. The dogs wagged their tails to see him, trotted close, but seemed to think better than to greet him. Instead, they shambled to the porch, giving him a wide berth.

Chapter Nine

Grace

The wagon lurched over the ruts in the road. While Grace found the trip tiring and uncomfortable, Abigail laughed heartily with each bump. The girl clapped her hands. Her face shone with happiness.

Grace noted that even Matt smiled at the girl's delight. Briefly. Just as quickly, his expression returned to one of stoic indifference. Every so often he'd cast a glance her direction. She felt herself wither each time. She knew he resented everything about her, but she couldn't allow him to bully her.

In the past, she'd avoided conversations with men. If her landlord wanted to discuss a repair, she wrote him a note, requesting he write her back. If her employer wanted to talk about her lace work, she found an excuse to attend the meeting with a friend or one of her sisters. Here in Texas, faced with Mr. Matt Bentley, she had no choice but to face him alone.

Neither spoke for the duration of the trip. What was there to say? He wanted her gone. She refused to do his bidding. With John's wealth, she might even be a woman of some means. Matt could try to tell her what to do, but he couldn't force her to do anything. John must have left money behind and once she knew more about the house, she'd see if there was money to support her and Abigail. Not for long, just long enough until Grace could find buyers for her lace work.

Surely the ladies in Texas liked to adorn their frocks with lace. She said a silent prayer that they did and added another prayer that she'd be able to make enough money to support herself and the child too.

The road climbed a ridge, offering a spectacular view. Cattle grazed in the green pastures. A river threaded through the hills like a silver ribbon. Clusters of trees grew along the banks.

"Texas is beautiful," she said, forgetting that she didn't really wish to speak to Mr. Bentley.

He obliged with a terse reply. "It is."

The trail turned towards a house set back in a grove of elm. The house, smaller than Matt's, looked older. No dogs greeted them. The farmyard was desolate. Grace couldn't suppress a shiver that came over her. Abigail grew quiet and suddenly Grace wondered if it might have been a mistake to bring her along. The house might hold bad memories for her. Grace didn't know if a small child would have much in the way of memories, bad or otherwise. The notion made Grace feel hollow inside. She and Abigail needed a home, but what if this place made the girl sad?

Matt brought the horses to a halt, set the brake and jumped down from the wagon. He hitched the horses and came to Grace's side for the baby. Grace handed her off and lowered herself down on the step.

"It's a lovely home," she said. "I hope that John and Mary were happy here."

"I believe they were. John never recovered from her death."

"I know that I came as a poor replacement, Mr. Bentley. You don't need to remind me."

"This might belong to you. Maybe. But this house is the house my brothers and I grew up in. If you try to sell it, you're in for a battle."

She shook her head. "It's not mine to sell. It's Abigail's birthright, but it's mine to *borrow.*"

Walking past him, she gave him a stern look, daring him to argue, praying he wouldn't. She went up the steps and pushed the front door open. Behind her Abigail fussed. The girl wanted to be in her arms, but Grace wanted Matt to hold her for a moment or two. To her surprise, Matt comforted the child. His tender tone made her turn to stare. She paused in the doorway and took in the sight of the tall, powerfully built man holding the small girl. Her heart squeezed with some emotion she couldn't name.

Abigail patted his face and smiled at him.

"You look surprised, Miss O'Brian."

"I am. A little."

He came up the steps and stood on the porch. She couldn't help retreating a half-step. Matt Bentley was head and shoulders taller than her. Standing a few paces from him made her realize just how much smaller she was.

"I care about Abigail. I didn't know she was being treated poorly by Bernice. I assumed John hired a good woman to tend to his child. I see now that I was wrong. No matter what happens, I'm grateful that you stepped in to help her."

Grace's jaw dropped.

"You don't believe me?"

"I do believe you. I just haven't heard you speak so many words all at once."

He pressed his lips together and narrowed his eyes. Despite his slightly ominous expression, Grace had the inexplicable urge to smile. He'd shown her a side of him she hadn't expected. He wasn't gruff and menacing *all* the time. He had a soft side.

Abigail patted his face again and cooed as if trying to soften his frown. He knit his brows and growled softly, making her giggle. He smiled, took her hand and blew raspberries on her palm.

Grace laughed softly, turned and pushed inside the house. Wandering from room to room, she took in the features of the house. Large windows allowed plenty of sunshine in, which pleased her. She imagined Hope and Faith sitting in the parlor, reading on a winter afternoon, basking in the sunlight. The furniture had been covered with sheets. She didn't bother looking under the protective covers. What did it matter? They'd had so little in Boston. Anything would be an improvement.

The kitchen was spacious, more room than she'd ever had. A large, circular table sat in the middle of the dining room. There were no chairs, but that would be an easy enough problem to fix. She paused for a long moment, trying to imagine her sisters sitting down to a meal.

Her eyes stung with tears. It seemed a lifetime since she'd seen Hope and Faith. If Mr. Bentley made problems for her, it might be quite some time before she could send for them. She turned away, grateful that Mr. Bentley was in a different part of the house and couldn't see her distress.

She found him on the front porch, talking to Abigail about a cardinal that chirped on a nearby tree.

"Where are all the animals?" she asked. "I thought John had a fair number of cattle."

He'd probably think she was being greedy. There was no helping the matter. She had to take care of practicalities, so she could eke out a life here in John's home.

"Most were sold in Fort Worth. The rest are grazing with the Bentley herd in the western pastures."

"There some money due then?"

She cringed, hating the way her words sounded.

His lips curved into a challenging smile. "Some."

"What's going to happen to the money?"

"I haven't decided."

"I believe a portion belongs to me." She folded her arms. "Or perhaps I should say, me and Abigail."

"What do you need money for? You live in my home."

She fumed. He was being deliberately thickheaded, tormenting her because that was the sort of horrid man he was. A moment before she'd been touched by how sweet he was with Abigail, but she'd been wrong. He wasn't a nice man. Not at all.

"I need money to pay for provisions and send for my sisters. I can earn money with my lace, but that will take some time. I don't intend to use John's money, or not if I can help it."

"Uh huh."

She bit her tongue to keep from lashing out at him with a sharp word. His smirk made her boiling mad. She wasn't the fighting type, Normally, she would shy away from any sort of confrontation, especially with a tall, obviously powerful man like Mr. Bentley, but she'd never had something so precious to fight for. Abigail inspired her to confront any difficulty. The need to protect the girl was at least as great as the need to help her dear sisters.

Fortunately, she had allies, people who might assist her. She returned his satisfied smile with one of her own. "Mr.

Bentley, I can ask Gus to take me to the bank and I'll find out myself."

His grin widened. "I'm sure that the banker, Mr. Calhoun, would take a shine to you. Especially if you have a little money coming your way."

"What difference does that make?"

"There's nothing Calhoun likes more than money and I'm not going to stand by while every man in Magnolia starts eyeing you and your property."

"But..."

"All the more reason for you to stay in my home. If you're out here, you'll have no end of gentlemen callers. They'll all be trying to court the pretty young widow, especially if she's rich too."

She shut the door behind her and strode past him. "Impossible man. Please take me home."

"What about our picnic?"

"I'll offer a bite to Abigail on the way home. I have no appetite."

"I could eat a horse."

Grace wanted nothing more than to return to the house, but Mr. Bentley insisted on the picnic. She followed him to a shady spot under an enormous oak tree. He carried the basket and held Abigail while he instructed her how to spread the picnic blanket.

"It's a little crooked on that edge," he said.

She straightened it and stood back. "How is that?"

"This side doesn't look quite right."

Pasting a smile to her lips she adjusted the blanket time and again until it was acceptable to him. She knew he toyed with her, probably trying to underscore how much of her life he controlled. By the time she sat down, she practically seethed with irritation, but when Abigail toddled over to her, arms outstretched, her annoyance vanished like dew on a summer's morning.

"My sweet girl," she murmured.

Harriet had packed sandwiches and a jar of lemonade. For dessert, she sent oatmeal cookies. Mr. Bentley continued to torment her throughout the lunch, making her either too irritated to respond, or making her laugh out loud at his presumptiveness. Every so often he complimented her on how she doted on Abigail, and in those moments, of course, she found him almost charming.

When they finished eating, Abigail stretched out on the blanket and promptly fell asleep.

"I'll take you to the bank soon, Miss O'Brian," he said quietly so as not to wake the child.

"I'm much obliged."

He regarded her with a curious look in his eye. She felt her skin warm under his scrutiny. What must he think of her, she wondered again. His moods were mercurial. One moment he seemed annoyed with her, other times he'd say something that was almost kind. She wanted him to think well of her. No, she needed him to think well of her. His life was intertwined with her life and that of Abigail.

"You grew up in this house?" she asked, hoping to have some sort of friendly conversation with him, a conversation that didn't turn into a debate.

He smiled, and the expression transformed his face. Matt Bentley was a handsome man, even if he thought his scar made him ugly. She didn't think for a minute it made him unattractive. Not that it mattered, of course.

"I grew up here and so did my father. My grandfather built the house when he married. He got the land because he fought in the Texas Revolution. They gave the soldiers 320 acres for every three months of service."

"Oh my," Grace said. A small thrill moved through her, pleasure that he was talking with her and telling her a little about the Bentley family.

"My grandfather got 1,280 acres. Since then, our family has added almost 10,000 more."

"I can hardly imagine." She turned her attention back to John's house. This was the house the Bentley brothers had grown up in. The notion filled her with warmth as she pictured the house bustling with the activity of a large family.

"Miss O'Brian, you could live in this home, if you had a husband. You'd be safe with a man caring for you."

His voice sent shivers down her back. What was this about? Did he mean to suggest the two of them? He'd said a few words about that last night, but now he looked at her in earnest. She held her breath.

He leaned back, sprawling across the blanket, crossing one ankle over the other and tucking his hands under his head. "If you had a husband, I wouldn't worry about you."

"A husband?"

"Right. I know just the man."

She swallowed hard, trying desperately to dislodge the lump in her throat. "You do?"

"I do. He's sweet on you. He hasn't said much, but I can tell."

She waited, a prickle of suspicion running across her skin.

He sighed. "It's Gus."

Oh, the man was a cad, teasing her like this. Her frantic heart slowed a little and the grip on her throat loosened as she watched his lips twitch. The smug look on his face was almost too much, but she schooled her features to give away nothing. Two could play this game.

"I'm afraid that won't work." It took tremendous effort to keep from smiling. Teasing Mr. Bentley pleased her more than it should. "I plan to propose to the banker-fellow you mentioned, Mr. Calhoun. I've heard he's terribly charming."

She didn't know anything about Mr. Calhoun, but some wicked inclination deep inside her couldn't resist teasing him right back.

Mr. Bentley's self-satisfied smile faded, and it was all she could do to keep from laughing at his indignation. She knew he was fibbing about Gus. The old-timer wasn't sweet on her. If anything, he seemed to fancy Harriet. Grace had seen the two of them exchange tender glances here and there.

Mr. Bentley might think she was just a silly young girl, but she hadn't fallen off the turnip wagon yesterday. She'd find a way to give him a taste of his own, unpalatable medicine.

Chapter Ten

Matt

Over the next few days, Matt kept busy, partly because there was plenty to do, and partly because he found time spent away from Grace was a little easier than time spent near Grace. She provoked him. Maybe not on purpose, but sometimes he wasn't sure.

When she wasn't provoking him, she distracted him terribly. She had an easy smile. She was pretty, very pretty, and her feminine presence made the house feel different. On one hand he felt almost like a stranger in his own house. He was very aware that it was presently her territory. On the other hand, he enjoyed coming home for meals and a chance to see her and Abigail.

She insisted that she should be in John's home. She seemed genuinely unhappy that she'd put Matt out of his home. Despite her desire to move to the old Bentley home, she refused to discuss the need to be married. Worse, the stubborn woman didn't even see the need to have a foreman on John's ranch. When he talked about having men around to keep an eye on things, she dismissed the idea out of hand.

"There are no animals on the ranch," she said one evening at dinner. "What would a foreman do with himself all day?"

"I don't know, Grace. But you're not living out there by yourself."

Arguments went round and round. For the life of him, he couldn't imagine Grace married to John. His brother would have lost patience with her long ago. John didn't care for people questioning his commands. Matt didn't care for it either, but something inside him felt a certain tenderness for Grace. He understood she wanted her own home. Didn't every woman? He admired the way she cared for Abigail. He'd never seen a happier child. She played happily every day. At night she fell asleep, exhausted and contented.

Grace was exhausted by the end of the day too. Abigail was just learning to walk. She often took a spill and Grace took it upon herself to follow her like a shadow, to try and keep her from tumbling.

Almost a week after he'd returned from Fort Worth, his brother Luke came to pay Grace and Abigail a call. He stopped by on his way back from town. They went to the sitting room to visit.

Grace blushed when she met him. "I won't stay long. Abigail is bound to get fussy."

"I want you to stay." Matt took the girl and stood by the window, so she'd have something to watch while they visited.

"I'm very sorry about your circumstances," Luke said. "Must have come as quite a shock."

"It was a shock," Grace said. "I'm so sorry John suffered. He wrote that he wasn't well, and I came as quickly as I could."

"That was mighty kind of you, Miss O'Brian. From what I've heard, Abigail's lucky to have you. We all are."

"Thank you. Abigail's such a joy. She's just started walking on her own."

Luke whistled as he turned his attention to Abigail. "Seems like she was just born yesterday."

"She's still a little wobbly. Sometimes I'm afraid I won't be able to keep her from hurting herself."

"Kids are tough," Luke said with a grin. "Won't be long and we'll need to get Abby a pony."

"I'm trying to convince your brother to help me move to John's home. I can't bear to think he's left his own house because of me."

Luke didn't respond right away. Matt figured it was because Luke was thinking what a bad plan that was. A woman couldn't live out in the country by herself. Why wouldn't she let go of that notion? Matt sighed. Stubborn woman. It must be true what they said about redheads. They were impossible.

"You can live there, if you want," Matt said, grudgingly. "But you'll need a foreman out there, and a few cowboys too. There's a bunkhouse. They could sleep there. There's plenty of work for them, they could mend the fence line."

"The barn's roof needs patching," Luke added. "I could spare a few men to work on that job."

"I hate to be a bother," Grace said. She paced by the chesterfield, stopped almost mid-stride and regarded them with dismay. "Or worse, a burden."

"You're not a burden," Luke said. "Don't think that for a minute."

Matt noticed Grace's shoulders lowered a fraction of an inch. She gave Luke a grateful smile. Matt frowned. For some reason, the smile she gave Luke made a flare of jealousy spark inside him. It was ridiculous. If Grace was sweet on Luke it might solve a few of his problems. At least he'd have his own bed back. Still, it bothered him.

"I'm sure you have plenty of work waiting, don't you, Luke?" His voice was a little sharper than he'd intended. Luke's lips tilted as his brows raised.

"I do?"

"Well – don't you?"

Luke got to his feet and offered his hand to Grace. "We're happy you're here. Remember that, even if my brother is as cantankerous as a mule."

Grace smiled at him. Again. Matt grumbled under his breath. Abigail patted his face. The sweet gesture was her response whenever he looked irritated. Until he'd started spending time with his niece, he'd never known how often he frowned. Maybe he was cantankerous.

He handed the girl back to Grace and showed his brother out. He stood on the porch and watched his brother ride off. The small knot of jealousy inside his chest unraveled a little. He didn't want to think too much about why it was there in the first place. It had to be because he felt protective of Grace.

A cry came from inside the house. It was Abigail. Matt ran inside and found Abigail and Grace in the hallway. Grace held the child, trying to console her. The girl wailed and clung to Grace. When her cries quieted, Grace was able to explain what had happened.

"She didn't want to hold my hand. She tripped and fell. I think it's her chin."

Matt held out his hands, but Abigail wouldn't be parted from Grace. She shook her head and sniffled. Tears stained her cheeks. A bruise darkened her chin.

"It's my fault." Grace's voice trembled. Her eyes filled with tears.

"Don't cry, Grace. We can't have two crying females in the house."

Harriet hurried down the hall. "I came as quickly as I could. Ooh, the poor lamb."

"I should have paid better attention," Grace said.

"Now, Miss O'Brian, there's no need being upset," Harriet soothed. "Children have little spills all the time. This isn't the first and it won't be the last, mark my words."

Matt offered to take Abigail again, and this time, she went to him. "Come on, girls, let me show you something in the barn. A little surprise."

He walked out of the house, held the door for Grace and led them to the barn. Both Grace and Abigail sniffled, but at least neither wept. The late afternoon light streamed through the windows, illuminating motes of dust. Abigail looked around wide-eyed.

"Listen, Abby. What do you hear?"

In the quiet of the barn a faint sound came from the back stall. Both she and Grace gave him tentative smiles. He took them to the back, unlatched the door and pointed to the kittens. Both Grace and Abigail murmured soft sounds of wonder.

The mother cat, a pretty calico, yawned and got up to greet them. She rubbed against Matt's leg as he crouched down with Abigail. She bumped against Abigail, purring loudly. The girl laughed and smiled up at Grace. She pointed at the kittens and prattled on with words that didn't make sense, but the joyful tone said all he needed to know.

Matt picked up one of the kittens and showed her how to stroke the tiny animal gently. It opened its mouth and made a small squeak. Grace crouched beside them and smiled as she watched Abigail.

He'd assumed the child would tire of the adventure, but she enjoyed it for far longer than he expected. When it was time to go home, he and Grace walked with Abigail between them, each holding one of her hands.

"Sometimes I worry that I shouldn't have taken her on," Grace said. "Maybe I should have found someone with more experience to care for Abigail."

Her words took him aback. She suggested she wasn't capable of caring for the girl? He'd never seen a woman who was more maternal and kinder and a hundred other wonderful things. If she'd said something like this when he'd first met her, he would have agreed heartily. Now he found himself disagreeing with her words. In just a short time she'd become part of his life, and Abigail's too. He'd never wanted to marry, didn't yearn for a wife, not like John. He'd seen how hard women had things when they took up with cattlemen. Even Mary, who was as tough and sturdy as any woman, had died soon after giving birth to Abigail.

They climbed the stairs slowly to give Abigail time to navigate each step.

"She's so small," Grace said. "So delicate. I worry all the time."

It was true. Abigail was small and delicate. He realized, with a start, that Grace's concerns about the child were the same as his concerns about Grace. At night, he'd lie awake, thinking about the harm that could befall Grace, the men that might prey upon her. Grace was good and kind and trusting, and there were men who would take advantage, or perhaps harm her.

The Sanders men hadn't troubled the Bentleys in some time, but the old wounds were there, festering. The hostilities could flare again, with the slightest provocation.

And yet, he didn't want her to go. Not anymore.

"You can't leave now." He gave her a teasing smile. "She's stuck with you, and you with her."

"I thought you wanted to be rid of me."

"We could just marry and be done with it." He'd spoken the words casually, but his intention was earnest. He felt the desire to marry her deep in his heart. Standing close to her in the quiet of the barn, he was overcome with the urge to pull her into his arms.

She shook her head. When he'd mentioned the idea in the past, she'd seemed irritated. Now she just looked downcast. "Thank you, Mr. Bentley, but I don't care to be your good deed. That's why I'm agreeing to living at John's home with the help of the foremen and cowboys, so I can leave you in peace."

"Is that so?"

"It is. Perhaps I could trouble you for one last favor."

He frowned, a surge of irritation coming over him. "Maybe. Depends what it is."

"Would you take me or allow Gus to take me to the bank? I'd like to understand Abigail's and my financial situation a little better. You'd mentioned that you would..."

Holding the front door open for her, he tried to keep from grumbling at her request. He didn't know how much money John had. He didn't begrudge Grace any of his brother's wealth. He didn't resent that she was the legal owner of John's house. What troubled him was the notion that once she saw the size of the bank balance, she'd set out on her own, emboldened and financed by John's money. And if she lived somewhere else, he wouldn't be able to protect her.

Chapter Eleven

Matt

A few days passed with an uneasy truce stretching between them. Matt found himself thinking of her more often than he liked. Often, he had a twinge of guilt about trying to control her circumstances. He didn't want to be the source of her unhappiness, but the need to protect her was as strong as anything he'd ever felt.

One afternoon, when he'd finished his tasks for the day, he saddled his chestnut gelding and headed out alone. He took the trail to John's house. A strange urgency had come over him, a nagging question about what John knew of Grace. He wasn't sure how much it mattered. John had been heart-broken when Mary died. Matt was certain his brother hardly thought of Grace, even though they'd exchanged letters.

He arrived at the old Bentley home, tied his horse to the hitching rail and went inside. The door creaked on rusted hinges, just another sign of his brother's neglect. Matt moved through the quiet house, past the furnishings draped in bed sheets and went to the office.

"John," he muttered. "You know I loved you. I wished I told you a few times, but I'm telling you now. I'm sorry. And I'm sorry for the tender feelings I have for Grace, but I can't help myself."

John, the old John, would have had a good laugh at him for talking to an empty house. His brother was seven years older than him and never tired of poking fun at his younger brother. All four Bentley boys could spend hours together, around a campfire, or the dinner table and argue, debate or generally give each other a hard time about just about everything.

Matt's heart twisted with pain as he stepped into his brother's study. The desk sat under a window in a spot of sunshine. A fine layer of dust covered the wood. He sat down, took the letter basket and found the envelope with the lock of hair.

Rifling through his brother's letters made him feel no better than a thief in the night. Despite his guilty conscience, he felt a surge of pleasure when he found the rest of the letters, bound by a ribbon. Slowly, he tugged the ribbon free. The letters spilled across the desk. Five of them. Three of them unopened.

He stared in disbelief. His brother hadn't even read all of Grace's letters. Picking up one of the unopened envelopes, he caught a hint of her scent. He sniffed the paper, greedy for more of her fragrance. Why would John ignore the letters? Matt knew if he'd received letters from Grace, he would have read them over and over. He grabbed the letter opener and moved to open the envelope, but hesitated.

An image of Grace came to him. He could almost see the hurt expression etched around her eyes. The letters weren't his to read. He itched to tear the envelope open and devour every single word she'd written from Boston. But no. He couldn't do that even though she'd never know. He'd know. And it would always bother him. He set the letter opener down.

The dilemma grew in his mind as he studied the assortment of notes. Were Grace to find out that John hadn't even opened and read her letters, she'd be hurt. Perhaps he could keep her from finding out. Thank goodness she hadn't come into the study the other day when they'd visited the house.

He wanted to shield her from that, but he was aware of less noble thoughts. A jealous twinge inside his chest. Even though John was his brother, his own flesh and blood, the resentment settled firmly inside him. He'd battled the same when Luke had smiled and flirted with Grace.

Grace is mine...

The thought came unbidden, but he felt the emotion keenly. Ridiculous. He wanted to marry her, of course, but it was to protect her, to give her a marriage of convenience. Or that's what he'd imagined. Now he wasn't so sure.

He tied the letters back into a small bundle. The sight of the small beribboned packet tugged at his heart. He knew the letters were filled with everything Grace had yearned for. He wanted to tuck them away, to protect the unread messages somehow as if he were protecting her. He slipped the bundle into his pocket, walked out of his brother's study and left the house.

As he rode home, his thoughts wandered to Grace and the discussion they'd had that morning. Their talk was a little more of a debate. As usual. She'd mentioned wanting to return to her lace work, so she could make her own way. He'd told her she didn't need to make her own way. That he'd always take care of her and Abigail. Her pale skin flushed a lovely pink when he said the words. He wasn't sure what strong emotion prompted her response. She looked flustered. He didn't want to cause her any upset, but he had to admit he liked making her blush.

He trotted into the barnyard, smiling at the memory.

Gus met him halfway, a solemn look on his face.

"What's wrong?" Matt asked.

"A couple of the neighbors are missing cattle. The Brewsters are down ten head. The O'Connells have lost all their older calves. They estimate twenty animals have been rustled."

Matt winced. The O'Connell's barn burned down last year. The young family was struggling mightily.

"Luke and Thomas told me right after you left. The three of us checked the back pasture. We counted seventy-five calves, two more than we expected. So good news, anyway."

Matt dismounted. A cowboy appeared in the barn doorway. He jogged over to take his horse from him. Matt handed him the reins silently, scrubbed a hand down his face and sighed with frustration.

"We've had a number of drifters moving through town," Gus said. "They probably helped themselves to some of the livestock. The youngsters wouldn't be branded just yet."

Matt nodded. "They're probably halfway to Fort Worth by now. Heading to the spring auction."

He scanned the house, seeking a glimpse of Grace. A feeling of foreboding came over him. It brought a certainty that he needed to keep her close. She sat on the porch swing. Abigail sat on her lap. Matt was too far away from the house to hear either of them, but he knew Grace was probably telling the child a story or singing her a song. Grace saw him watching her and waved.

He lifted his hand and waved back. He tried to give the air of nonchalance even though dread weighed heavily in his heart. The thieves might be gone. Or they might be hiding out around Magnolia, looking for more trouble.

Chapter Twelve

Grace

While Matt had agreed to take her to the bank, Grace realized several days later that he hadn't said when. The subject came up over dinner a time or two. He worked hard to change the subject or put her off. He toyed with her, dismissed her plans and often, late at night when the house was quiet, she'd summon every last ounce of indignation she could. It never amounted to much.

There were two reasons for that. The first was that her sisters had written to say they'd found a better boarding house. They were no longer subject to the landlord's violent outbursts. A room had come available with the sister of their pastor. Grace felt sure that Faith and Hope were in good hands with Mrs. Hutchison.

The second reason Grace couldn't ever stay angry with Matt was the way he doted on her and Abigail. It was as if he wanted her to stay in his home. He'd surprise her in so many ways with small kindnesses. One night he came to dinner with a bunch of daisies for her and a tiny turtle for Abigail. He showed her how the small creature tucked his head into his shell, and the two would watch, waiting for it to push its head back out.

Then there was the morning where he came to the house, just before breakfast, to show them where a doe grazed in the orchard. A newborn fawn tottered behind her. Abigail had watched in silence, completely entranced by the tiny creature.

Every day it seemed, Grace witnessed some new, astonishing sight. Animals and birds, majestic sunsets, powerful storms. Texas was a whole new world to her. She was content, for the most part, missing only her sisters and a place she could call her own.

Not that it was a terrible trial to live in Mr. Bentley's home. She saw him several times a day. Each time her heart would leap up. She'd find herself thinking about him when he was away and wondered if he ever thought about her. At times, she found him gazing at her, a curious expression lighting his eyes. She loved those small, stolen moments and relived them in her mind. Thoughts of him always stirred a yearning inside her.

Other times, Matt seemed preoccupied with some worry. She tried to coax the reason from him. He put her off, saying it was nothing, just the usual business of ranching. Still, she had the feeling that there was more going on than he let on. In the evenings, he'd retire to his study with Luke and Thomas. The three Bentley brothers would talk, in low, solemn tones and it seemed that their conversations were more serious than simple ranch concerns.

She found excuses to seek him out. When he'd brought a herd of cattle in from the one of the back pastures, she took Abigail to the corral to watch him work. Clad in his cowboy attire and wearing his chaps and cowboy hat, he cut a heroic image. He rode his horse amidst the churning mass of cattle. He and his animal moved as if they were one.

When he'd completed the task, he directed the other men to push the young animals into a holding pen. He went on to tell them that he'd take the remaining cattle back out to pasture. Before he left, he turned in the saddle and directed his gaze at her. The brim of his hat cast a shadow over his eyes, but his gaze affected her nonetheless.

The days passed, one easing into the next. She was so taken with Abigail and the easy cadence of her life, she hardly noticed how quickly time passed. It was almost three weeks since she'd arrived, when she addressed his reluctance to take her to the bank. They sat together, the three of them, eating a fine stew Harriet had prepared.

"Mr. Bentley, I wonder if I could trouble you to take me into town." Her stomach knotted but she forged ahead. "Perhaps in the morning. Mrs. Patchwell has offered to watch Abigail while I attend to the business of the bank."

A flicker of irritation passed behind his eyes. "I suppose."

She turned away and spoke softly to Abigail, telling her what a good girl she was for eating the stew's vegetables. The child wore a great deal of the stew on her chin and bib. She held up a pea for Grace to inspect, then popped it in her mouth, grinned and clapped her hands. She ate a tiny cube of potato and applauded her own efforts.

Grace couldn't help but smile at the girl's antics. Still, she felt a twinge of guilt for asking anything of Mr. Bentley. She knew he was terribly busy, but how could she move forward without his help? It was as if he wanted to keep her from leaving.

"I often feel as though I should apologize to you. Not only have you lost your brother, but you're saddled with his child and, er... wife."

He grumbled under his breath. "You can't really claim to be his wife. Not fully. Let's not pretend that the two of you were a couple."

"Will you fight me over Abigail's inheritance?"

"Not unless you act recklessly."

"Have I acted recklessly?"

"Not yet."

"But you assume I will."

"You don't know about running a ranch, and you might not know how to run a house while caring for a little one."

"I'm not a child," she snapped.

Abigail's mouth formed a perfect circle. "Uh-oh."

Grace stared in amazement, unsure of what she'd heard. Had the girl just said her first word? Part of her felt a twinge of disappointment. How would it feel to have the girl call her 'mama'? She had no right to be addressed as 'mama' but her heart yearned to hear the word. Instead Abby had said 'uh-oh'. It struck Grace as an apt commentary on the entire predicament.

Uh-oh, indeed.

"I know you're not a child, Grace," he said. "But you're a woman who grew up in Boston. Have you ever seen a rattlesnake?"

"I haven't."

"And if you did?"

"I'd walk the other direction."

He sighed. "What about a mountain lion?"

"I didn't know there are mountain lions here."

"There are."

Her gaze drifted to the scar on the side of his face. "I suppose I should learn how to shoot a gun."

Mr. Bentley narrowed his eyes and looked even more irked. She could see he was preparing a long-winded lecture on needing a man around to take care of things. It was a point she didn't deny, but she was certain even if she agreed to a regiment of able-bodied men, he'd find an argument against her living in John's home.

"I'm merely trying to vacate your home so that you may return. I'm certain you don't enjoy sleeping in the barracks."

"Barracks!" He snorted. "It's a bunkhouse, not a military camp."

There it was again, his condescending attitude. One moment he could be as kind as could be, and another moment, he could be the most tiresome, impossible man she'd ever known.

"Just the same, I'm sure you prefer the quiet and the comfort of your own bedroom at night. I can't imagine sleeping with a dozen men."

The moment the words came from her mouth, she wished them back. A rush of warmth flooded across her skin. Her cheeks burned, and she fixed her gaze on her stew, refusing to look at him. She could feel his intent gaze and imagined his smirk as he enjoyed her discomfort.

He chuckled. "Mighty glad to hear that, Miss O'Brian."

She could hear the smile in his voice. Squeezing her eyes shut for a moment, she tried to tamp down her mortification. If he wanted to, he could tease her endlessly about such a comment. Drawing a deep breath, she opened her eyes, straightened and reached for another roll. She buttered it and shot him what she hoped was an imperious look.

He grinned. "It's not a lot of fun sleeping in the same cabin as a bunch of sweaty, smelly, bad-mannered cowboys. Some nights I don't get a wink of sleep, or that's what it feels like. The whole crew, all of them snore and grumble and fart."

Grace stared in disbelief. He'd never used any sort of coarse language around her. Immediately he flushed, his cheeks reddening with embarrassment.

Abigail chuckled. She held up a pea, popped it in her mouth and clapped. "Ha, ha! Fa!"

She resumed eating, ignoring the two adults.

"You must feel so proud, Mr. Bentley." Grace bit her lip to keep from laughing. She enjoyed his mortification as much as he'd enjoyed hers. Turnaround being fair play and all that. "You've taught Abigail her second word."

Mr. Bentley looked sheepish. "I'd be happy to take you into town in the morning, Miss O'Brian. Just let me know when it suits you."

Chapter Thirteen

Matt

Going to town had to be postponed another day, however. The morning dawned, and a rider arrived to tell Matt that Luke and Thomas's foreman's wife had given birth. Harriet was often called upon to help young mothers. Thomas had sent word, wondering if Matt could spare her.

The house was thrown into a flurry of activity. Both Harriet and Grace worked in the kitchen to prepare food to take. Matt was impressed with how not only did Grace not say a word of complaint about postponing the bank visit, she joined Harriet in her efforts.

She worked while Abigail napped or sat in her high chair munching on a soda cracker. The kitchen smelled wonderful. Matt remarked several times as he passed through but stopped after Harriet frowned.

"You don't care to share your kitchen," he teased.

"It's fine," Harriet sniffed. "Miss O'Brian knows her way around a kitchen. I'll give her that."

Grace gave him a remorseful look. "I'm trying to stay out of the way."

He drove Harriet, Grace and Abigail to Luke and Thomas's section of the ranch that afternoon. Harriet disappeared into the foreman's house, while Matt and Grace unloaded the provisions. Thomas rode up and offered to lend a hand.

“Harriet must have been cooking all night,” Luke said.

Matt set the pie basket on the counter. “Grace helped.”

Thomas’s brows lifted. “Harriet Patchwell let another woman in her kitchen? Did you have to defend yourself with a chair and whip?”

Grace laughed and scooped Abigail into her arms, setting the child on her hip. “I don’t think she thought I knew how to cook. I made the cottage pie and the lemon cake.”

“A pretty lady who knows how to cook like an angel,” Thomas marveled as he smiled at her.

Matt felt the sudden urge to whisk Grace away from his admiring glance. It was true. Grace was a pretty lady, but he still resented his brother or any man noticing. Most of all he wanted her to be his and to feel the same way he did. He didn’t simply want a marriage of convenience. The realization hit him hard. Where had it come from? He wasn’t the marrying kind. He reeled from the shock, realizing that suddenly he’d become the very thing he’d never imagined. He wandered to the window and pictured Grace living in his home permanently. How could he convince her, though? Especially since he hadn’t been particularly welcoming when they first met.

Behind him, Grace chatted with Thomas. Matt kept his gaze fixed on the horizon as he tried to reconcile the turmoil of his thoughts.

“My mother taught me and my sisters how to cook several Irish dishes,” she said. “Meals she’d grown up eating in Dublin. I enjoy cooking.”

“From the aroma, I’m sure you’re very good,” Thomas said.

Matt muttered under his breath and turned back to face them. “Don’t you have something you need to do?”

"No." Thomas said the word absent-mindedly while he kept his gaze fixed on Grace.

Grace eyed him too, a sly smile playing on her lips. "My sisters are both far better cooks than I am."

Matt snorted. He knew where this was going. Grace was going to play match-maker to get around his order that her sisters couldn't come to Texas. She looked over at him and gave him a mischievous grin.

Returning her attention to Thomas, she went on. "And, in truth, I'm considered the plain one in the family."

Thomas's jaw dropped, drawing a deep round of laughter from Matt.

She turned and gave him a look of wide-eyed innocence. "Truly."

He shook his head and she dismissed him with a wave of her hand.

"Don't you need a helpmeet?" she asked Thomas.

Thomas drew a deep breath. "Oh... well, I'm not sure about that. I don't think I'm the marrying type. I had my heart broken long ago. I figured marriage isn't for me."

Grace's face fell. The kitchen grew quiet. Abigail looked around and said a soft, 'uh-oh'.

"I'm sorry, Thomas," Grace said hurriedly. "I was mostly teasing. Matt's been so adamant that I not send for my sisters. I was being terribly forward."

Thomas shook his head. "It's fine."

Grace's face was pale, and she looked to Matt imploringly. Matt knew she felt terrible. It wasn't her fault, of course. He should have told her before about the circumstances. There was more to the story than Thomas let on, but now wasn't the time.

Harriet came into the kitchen. "Mr. Bentley, they'd like me to stay the day if that's all right with you?"

"Of course," Matt said.

"I can take Harriet back this evening," Thomas offered.

"All right," Matt agreed.

Grace and he said their goodbyes. Thomas walked them out to the wagon and the two men talked about the new calves that had been born that spring. Matt noticed that Grace listened with interest. He wondered if she would want to have a hand in any of the cattle business. By rights, a fourth of it was hers, unless she married. The thought bothered him plenty even though he didn't expect she was looking for a new husband. She only wanted to be near Abigail. He was certain of that. Mostly certain, anyway.

Doubt gnawed at him. They got into the wagon and he helped Grace up while Thomas held Abigail. Earlier when she ascended the wagon, she'd done so on her own while he held Abby. This was the first time he'd clasped her waist. He hadn't missed the sharp intake of her breath when he touched her, or the narrow expanse of her delicate frame.

He set her on the seat and she gave him a bewildered look. Panic flared in her eyes. Unable to hold his gaze, she looked away.

Curling his hands into fists, he yearned to touch her again. He didn't dare. He knew better. She was a young and vulnerable woman and he was, for now, her protector. He wouldn't allow himself to take liberties. Grace depended on him and he was determined to care for her as she deserved. That didn't mean he wouldn't try to convince her that she should accept a proposal from him. One day.

Thomas held Abigail. The two exchanged a smile as Thomas jiggled her a little to amuse her. Abigail clapped her hands with delight.

“What a little sweetheart,” Thomas said. “She favors Mary, doesn’t she?”

The instant he said the words, he gave Grace a look of remorse. “I’m sorry. Maybe I shouldn’t have mentioned Abby’s mother.”

Grace shook her head and grew thoughtful. “Why would I mind? It doesn’t bother me in the least. I know that I’m just a poor replacement for Mary. I feel blessed to witness any part of her childhood. Abigail should hear stories about her parents, since she won’t ever know them any other way.”

Matt found himself watching her as she spoke. He noted the quiet dignity, the selflessness and the way she kept her gaze fixed on the child. It remained there until she finished speaking and then she stole a glance at him. A blush bloomed across her pale skin as she turned away. He smiled as he watched her pale skin turn a lovely pink. His smile faded as he realized Thomas was smiling at Grace too, giving her an admiring look.

“We’d best go,” Matt said, his voice gruffer than he intended.

Thomas handed up the child. “I’m sure little Abby is equally blessed. Speaking of blessings, thank you for the food you sent. I’m going to make a point to stop by my foreman’s home for dessert this evening. I think I need to sample some of that lemon cake.”

Grace nodded. “I hope you find it to your liking.”

“I’m sure that I will,” Thomas said.

Matt felt a shot of annoyance course through his veins. It irked him that Thomas would sample Grace’s baking before he'd ever tasted a single bite. All the way over to his brothers' ranch, the tantalizing fragrance of the lemon cake had tempted him and made his mouth water. He wanted a taste, especially because Grace had made it. Now Thomas would enjoy it and he would have nothing.

There was something about Grace that made him jealous. He felt petty and resentful. Like he was a lovesick boy who couldn't control his emotions. It wasn't anything he'd experienced before. He didn't like it. Not at all.

He scowled at his brother. Thomas grinned, clearly enjoying his distress. Thomas directed his attention to Grace, giving her a winning smile.

"So glad you've come to Magnolia, Miss O'Brian," Thomas said. "Our family is more grateful than you can know."

Chapter Fourteen

Grace

The next morning, Matt hitched the wagon to take Grace into town. It was a fine, cloudless day. Grace might have been pleased, but it was the first time Grace had been apart from Abigail. She missed her even before she'd left the ranch, even though Abigail was in good hands. Harriet had been more than happy to set aside her chores to care for the child.

The first little while they rode together in silence. Grace couldn't think of what to say, and Mr. Bentley seemed preoccupied. As they rode through a valley he startled her by pointing out a patch of flowers.

She yelped in surprise and then laughed at her own foolishness. "I'm sorry, Mr. Bentley. What were you saying?"

His lips quirked. "Those flowers over there are called Bluebonnets. That's the first I've seen this year. Soon they'll be blooming as far as the eye can see."

Grace held her hat as a breeze stirred. She scanned the surrounding pastures. Pale blue flowers dotted the land. The breeze moved over the grasses, turning the fields into rolling waves of green. "So beautiful. I wish Abigail were with us."

"We can take her out for a little ride again, if you like."

She sighed, not sure if she dared look forward to an outing with him. Several times that morning, he'd looked at her and made her heart race wildly. And then his shoulder brushed hers a time or two, making her thoughts scatter like frightened rabbits. Mr. Bentley rendered her usual calm disposition into that of a giddy schoolgirl.

Suddenly she realized he awaited her answer to his offer to take her out again.

She blushed. "I'm certain Abigail would like that very much."

"What about you?"

Her cheeks flamed. "I would like it as well."

He smiled, his eyes sparking with amusement. The man clearly enjoyed making her blush. She shook her head and looked away.

"Do you like it here?" he asked.

His question surprised her. Searching his eyes, she tried to determine if he were teasing her or in earnest. His expression was thoughtful, not teasing.

"I love it here." Her voice trembled with a wave of emotion she hadn't seen coming.

"I'm glad."

They drove a while longer and then he added, "I'm glad you're here."

Warmth filled her chest. She smiled, unable to resist teasing him a little to get back at him. "You're being especially charming this morning. Is it because I might be a rich woman? You're trying to gain my favor?"

"I guess I'd better mind my manners if you're inheriting a fortune. Are you thinking of all the fine things you can buy?"

He was teasing her. Again. Resolving to teasing him right back, she nodded. "So many fine things. I'll have a butler. *Finally.*"

His smile widened. "Good idea. Every rich lady needs one of them."

"Perhaps some ladies in waiting while I'm at it. And I'll have season tickets to the Magnolia Theater."

He laughed. "I'm sorry, ma'am. Magnolia has about ten places of business but no theater."

She waved her hand. "I shall build one, then. A grand and glittering venue. I'll call it The Abigail."

He held her in his gaze. "Is that what you'd like? Theaters and butlers?"

"No, Mr. Bentley," she said quietly. "I just want my sisters to come, and I want them to come before the winter."

"Why is that?"

She drew a sharp breath. Usually when she mentioned the subject of her sisters, Mr. Bentley dismissed the idea of out hand. Today he was actually asking about them. This was progress, indeed.

"My sister Faith gets very ill every winter. The work houses are damp and musty and always cold. I don't want them to work there anymore. That's the reason I first thought of writing to John. So, I could come to Texas, to try to make a way for them."

He nodded. "I see."

She wondered if he did, or if he was just humoring her. They said little else until they arrived in town. Mr. Bentley took the horse and wagon to the livery while she perused the goods in the mercantile. The shopkeeper asked if she needed any help, making her wish she'd brought a sample of her lace work. She examined the fabric display. Bolts of material lined the shelves like so many library books. Her fingers itched to touch the gauzy, delicate silk and the soft, breezy linen.

Abigail had a number of little dresses, but they were all so drab. Grace longed to make something pretty for the little girl. Something light and summery. Perhaps a few bonnets as well.

If she could manage to spare some of her lace, she'd adorn Abigail's little frocks with a lace collar or hem. The idea made her eyes prickle with tears of happiness. How sweet her girl would look in a colorful dress.

She wandered out of the shop and admired the fine dishes displayed in the window. She hadn't had time to look through John's kitchen and wondered how well it was stocked. How odd it felt to imagine a stranger's house. Soon, she hoped, she would walk into the house and make it her own. Everything in it had been brought in by John and Mary, two people she'd never met and yet to whom she was intimately connected. A pang of discomfort twisted inside her chest.

What she was doing was right. That's what she told herself. She was taking the house and the possessions of Mary and John Bentley, so she could care for their daughter. Drawing a deep breath, she squared her shoulders and tried to set aside her misgivings.

A woman passed her on the boardwalk and turned down a side street. Grace had only seen her from the back, but she wore a dress made of a vibrant red material. Her skirts swished as she went around the corner. Grace turned back to the mercantile's window display, but her attention was drawn by the glint of something shiny. She bent over and picked up a small pearl earbob.

"Miss," she called. She hurried around the corner just in time to see the woman vanish through the side door of a building.

Grace rushed down the alley and knocked on the door. A moment later, a man answered. He wore a suit and tie and was dressed respectably, but he gave her a lingering look that made her take a step back. It was indecent, and she gave a small huff of surprise.

"I don't believe I know you."

"No," she said stiffly. "We haven't met."

His lips curved into a smile. "Now we have."

Music came from inside the building. Someone played the piano. Amidst the din, she heard laughter and people talking in raised voices. It dawned on her that this was a pub. In Texas, they called them saloons. Either way, they were no place for a lady. Brushing her discomfort aside, she held out her hand to show him the small pearl. "A lady just passed by and entered this building."

"Yeah. I know."

"She dropped an earbob. Would you kindly return it to her?"

"All right." He took the pearl from her, dragging his fingers across her palm. "What's your name?"

His tone and demeanor frightened her. She yanked her hand back and turned without a word. Behind her, the man laughed and slammed the door shut. She glanced back to make sure he wasn't following. Thankfully, he remained inside the building. Hurrying up the alley, she felt a wave of urgency to return to the busy boardwalk. A few dozen paces from the end of the alley a man appeared before her. Another man joined him, blocking her way.

A shiver of fear rippled across her skin. She was in a grimy alley. Alone. Even if she screamed for help, no one would hear.

"Aren't you a pretty little thing."

"I don't think we've seen you before. You one of the new girls at the saloon?"

Grace opened her mouth but could summon no reply.

The men stepped closer. "I don't think she's one of the new girls, Jed. I think she looks too highfalutin'. Besides, she was just talking to Bentley. He don't consort with any of the saloon girls."

Grace retreated several steps, too frightened to speak.

"Too good to even say hello."

One of the men, the shorter of the two, turned his head to spit. He wiped his mouth with his sleeve and resumed leering at her. The other rubbed his jaw and licked his lips.

"Please let me pass," she finally managed. "I have business to attend."

"Aw, c'mon, honey. We'd like to get to know you a little better. How come you're so unfriendly?"

"I don't know who you are."

"I'm Jeb Sanders and he's my brother, Frank. That's 'bout all you need to know. What's your name?"

She shook her head. Words failed her. The Sanders family... she'd heard of them, but never imagined coming face to face with any of them. The two men were far worse than her most terrifying nightmare.

"The girl's got some bad manners."

"Maybe we ought to school her in how to talk polite."

"You a friend of Matt Bentley?"

"Didn't think that ugly cuss would ever have such a pretty sweetheart."

They moved closer. She backed away from them, wishing desperately she could make some sort of sound. A cry for help. A scream. Anything. But her throat was too tight to make a sound. She was helpless, just like in all her nightmares.

Suddenly the taller of the two men was jerked from his feet. It was as if a giant force yanked him in the air. Mr. Bentley loomed behind the two men. He gripped the taller one by the collar and threw him against the brick wall. The man hit the bricks with a sickening thud, groaned and sank to the ground, not moving again. Mr. Bentley lunged at the other. He grabbed the man by the front of the shirt and threw a hard punch. His fist connected with the man's jaw and he crumpled to the ground as well.

Mr. Bentley's eyes burned with fury. He moved closer, his gaze raking over her. "Did they touch you?"

Grace had never seen a man so possessed by fury. Every instinct inside her urged her to get away from him, but her feet were rooted to the ground. He cupped her shoulders and for a moment said nothing as he searched her face.

"I'm f-fine," she stammered.

"Are you hurt?"

She shook her head.

"Why did you come down here?"

"I had to..." her words trailed off.

His anger shocked her almost as much as the filthy intentions of the rough men who lay motionless and bloody on the ground. She shook, trembling like a new leaf in a spring storm. Holding up her hands, she implored him silently.

"Gracie," he said in a softer tone. "Gracie... sweetheart." He dropped his hands and backed away from her. "Never mind. It doesn't matter. I shouldn't have left you alone. My fault."

Chapter Fifteen

Matt

Sitting inside the bank president's office, Matt's blood boiled with white-hot rage. The Sanders boys had followed Gracie. His Gracie. And they would have hurt her just to get back at the Bentley family. Grace was shaken by the experience. Thoroughly. It dawned on him that she was just as afraid of him as she was afraid of the men who had accosted her.

Grace considered him to be as bad as the Sanders brothers. The thought sickened him.

Another time, the thought might have drawn an apology from him, but right now, he saw the value of making an impression on her. She'd resisted his help every time he offered. Stubborn girl. She couldn't know that there were other men in Magnolia just like Jeb and Frank. Men who preyed on single women, and he intended to do whatever he needed to keep Grace safe. As he sat in the office, waiting for Baron Calhoun, he began to form a plan. He needed to make Grace his. Sooner rather than later.

Baron Calhoun strode into the office and shook his hand. "Nice to see you, Matt."

Matt nodded. He had a grudging respect for Baron. The man owned several Magnolia businesses. Folks said he had the Midas touch. He was a man of business but a rancher too, running a spread to the east of Magnolia that rivaled that of the Bentley Brothers.

"Baron," Matt said with a curt nod, shaking the man's hand.

"Sorry to hear about John," Baron replied. "Your brother was a fine man."

"Much obliged." Matt withdrew his hand. He glanced at the back of his hand, noting a scrape across the knuckles.

Baron gave him an inquisitive look.

"A little run-in with the Sanders," Matt said.

Baron's look darkened but he said nothing. Matt knew the man shared his feelings about the Sanders boys. The man might dress in a fine suit, but Baron Calhoun was known to brawl a time or two.

Baron shook his head and the two men exchanged a knowing look. This wasn't the time or place to talk about scum like the Sanders. Grace stood, pale and shaken. Baron gave her a sympathetic look as he took her hand in his. He said a few words of condolence, moved to his desk and sat down.

They chatted for a few moments about Grace's trip to Texas. Baron asked her how she liked Magnolia and living in the countryside. Grace regained some of her composure. Color returned to her face and when she spoke of Abigail, she smiled a little.

"Grace takes wonderful care of John's daughter," Matt said. "You've never seen a happier child."

Grace gave him an appreciative smile.

Baron nodded. "I'm glad to hear it. About John's account... I'm sure you'll forgive me for being blunt and to the point. You know that John wasn't well in his last few months of life. He's left a few debts behind."

"I knew he had some troubles, but I wasn't aware of the debts."

Grace's eyes widened.

"And of course, there's the issue of Grace and John's marriage," Baron said. "The signature on the proxy does not match the signature on any of John's papers."

Matt leaned back in his chair, not sure what to think about that. His brother hadn't been thinking straight for a long time. Could his confusion have caused him to sign his name differently?

Grace gripped the armrests of the chair, her knuckles growing white. She turned to him with wide, terror-filled eyes. "Mr. Bentley," she whispered. "I hope you don't think I forged John's signature. Why would I do such a thing?"

He almost smiled at the notion. "No, I don't think you're a forger, Grace. That's the last thing I'd consider."

"There might be a copy of the proxy in John's home," Baron went on. "Perhaps with the letters you exchanged. You would do well to look for it. However, even if it's found, I'm not sure it will be regarded as a legal document. The Bentley brothers could challenge your marriage in court."

Grace lifted her trembling hand to her lips. "No... it can't be."

"I'm afraid that's where things stand, ma'am." Baron folded his hands and regarded Grace with pity in his eyes.

"I love Abigail," she said softly. "I want to care for her. That's all. I don't need the money. I can make my own way."

Baron blinked. "How so?"

"I'm a seamstress and a lace-maker. I can do either. Or both." She bit her lip and shook her head. "This can't be. I can't be parted from her."

"Abigail loves you," Matt said. "No one's going to part the two of you."

He got to his feet and held out a hand to Grace. She stared at it for a moment and then set her hand in his. He helped her up and kept his hold on her hand.

"Thank you, Baron," Matt said. "My brothers and I will help Grace sort things out. You've been more help than you know."

Baron knit his brow and scratched his head. "I have?"

"You have. We'll get going. Grace has had a difficult day."

"Certainly, I will send a letter with a complete accounting of John's accounts within the week."

Baron saw them out. Matt kept Grace's hand in his as he ushered her out of the bank. They walked along the boardwalk without speaking. She wore an expression of stunned disbelief.

Later, when they'd driven the buckboard out of the hustle and bustle of Magnolia, Matt spoke. "You were almost badly hurt today, Grace."

"I know. I'm sorry." She spoke quietly, her tone flat.

"You don't need to apologize for anything. You just need to understand that Magnolia is a sight different than Boston."

She gave him a sharp look.

"Never mind. What I want to say is that I'm offering for you, Grace. You and I can marry and give a home to Abigail. I'll settle John's debts."

When she didn't answer right away, he gripped the reins a little tighter. Gritting his teeth, he tried to school his temper as he thought of the two men looming over Grace. That morning when he'd seen them threatening Grace, his temper snapped. It was all he could do to keep from killing the men. Even now, the idea of ending them filled him with primitive satisfaction.

"One shouldn't marry out of a sense of obligation," she said. "It's not a good reason."

"It's a perfect reason," he growled.

She lifted her chin and looked away.

"Grace, you are the most impossible woman I've ever met."

"Then I won't impose a lifetime of misery on you."

They went on another mile. He shot her a few furious looks. She maintained her haughty stance. With her lips pursed, shoulders squared and her back ram-rod straight, she looked like the very picture of obstinacy. He was glad that she no longer looked terrified. Plenty of women would have dissolved into hysterics if they'd suffered such a scare. Grace was stronger than she knew. But she was stubborn and exasperating too.

He wanted to stop the wagon, pull her into his arms and kiss that disapproving mouth. He'd wanted to kiss her before, but never with such desire as he felt now. Why that was he couldn't say. Probably because she was digging deep under his skin, irritating him to hell and back.

He imagined the look of outrage on her face if he stole a kiss. Would she slap him? He rubbed his jaw, thinking about her hand connecting with his face. He glanced at her and let his gaze fall to her lips. The idea of claiming them one day cooled his ire. He smiled. She noticed and flinched.

"You can't live in a house by yourself," he said gruffly. "I won't allow it."

She rolled her eyes. His gaze drifted back to her pouting lips. He had to force himself to look away. Grace was beautiful. Determined and fiery. He wanted to shield her from every possible threat. And he wanted to keep her as his own.

"If I agree to marry you, will you send for my sisters?"

He shook his head. "Maybe. But not right away. First off, I need to take care of you."

She said nothing, but it was clear from the fire in her eyes, she was thinking plenty.

"Grace," he said quietly. "What if you'd been walking down that alley with Abigail in your arms?"

The wagon lurched over a rut. She grabbed his arm and clung to him but pulled her hand away when the wagon returned to even ground. To his dismay, she lifted her hand to her eyes and wiped a tear.

Remorse twisted inside him. He wanted to offer her what he assumed all women wanted. Pretty words and wooing and all the things she deserved. Instead he was railroading her into a marriage with him, the same day she'd almost been assaulted. He grimaced but said nothing. It had to be done.

"All right," she said in a small voice that was choked with tears. "I'll marry you, Mr. Bentley."

Chapter Sixteen

Grace

The two days passed with little spoken about the wedding. Matt had discussed his wishes with his brothers and they'd agreed to make arrangements. He asked her if she needed anything, but she'd brought a wedding dress from Boston. Shoes, too. She had everything for the day of the wedding.

She wrote a letter to her sisters. Instead of long passages about the wonders of Texas, the wide-open spaces, the strange assortment of animals, like armadillos and the like, she wrote just a few lines. She told them Matt had offered for her. She'd accepted. It was for the best. Marriage would provide a home for Abigail and she hoped to send for them before the fall.

Instead of fretting about the upcoming wedding, Grace kept busy with Abigail.

The third morning after the incident in town, the two were confined to indoors. Thunder rumbled around the ranch. Harriet warned her of bad weather. She came to the sitting room with tea for Grace.

Grace watched Abigail as the child walked unsteadily along the edge of the chesterfield, at times holding the cushions for balance, other times taking a few steps on her own. The girl glanced over her shoulder and grinned at Grace and Harriet. Both women clapped and praised her efforts.

"Look how grown up you are," Harriet announced. "Such a big girl."

Grace clasped her hands in front of her. There were times when she could hardly tear her eyes from Abigail. Part of her relished every little milestone, and part of her wanted to keep the girl just as she was.

"One day you'll have one of your own," Harriet said.

"God willing, but Abigail *is* mine. I feel it in my heart."

Harriet nodded. "I wanted to ask you something about the wedding. I'd give anything to see your dress. If you're willing."

Grace blushed. "I'd love to show you."

She darted into the parlor and took the dress from where it hung on the back of the door. When she returned to the sitting room, she crossed to the window and draped the dress across a chair. Fluffing the skirts, she tried to show off the lace work.

"My sisters and I did the lace work together. The dress makes me feel like a little part of them is here with me." Her hand moved to her collar, where her locket hung under the trim. Suddenly, her breath caught in her throat. She hurried to pick up Abigail, so she could fend off the tears that threatened to spill from her eyes.

"My, my," Harriet marveled. She stared at the dress in wonder, gaping until she finally lifted her gaze to Grace. "It's the prettiest thing I've ever seen."

"Thank you. I'll wear a veil too."

"Tell me it's lace as well."

"Yes."

Harriet's eyes misted. "I feel like my own daughter's getting married."

"Don't cry, Harriet. You'll make me cry."

"You're missing your sisters. Of course, you are."

"I promised I'd do everything in my power to bring them to Texas."

Harriet pursed her lips together, moved to the door and closed it softly. "I shouldn't say anything."

Grace couldn't imagine what she was talking about, but if it pertained to her sisters, she needed to know. She closed the distance between them and spoke in a hushed tone. "Tell me, Harriet. Don't leave me wondering."

"Mr. Bentley spoke with his brothers about your sisters. Both sounded intrigued and I wondered if Luke or Thomas might write and offer for them."

Grace's jaw dropped. Matt had been dead set against her sisters coming. He'd changed his mind. It was a miracle.

Abigail squirmed in her arms, but when she saw Grace's expression she grew interested. Laughing, she patted Grace's chin. "Uh-oh."

Grace took her hand and kissed it and then turned her attention back to Harriet. "You wouldn't toy with me, would you?"

Harriet narrowed her eyes. "Certainly not. What do you take me for?"

"I wonder why he didn't want to tell me."

Harriet threw an exasperated gaze to the ceiling and then back to Grace. "He didn't want to get your hopes up, that's why."

"How kind of him," Grace murmured.

"That man is over the moon for you."

A strange feeling settled over her. She hadn't imagined he had any feelings for her whatsoever. From the beginning she felt like a burden or obligation. One day, they walked through the barnyard and the dogs came to greet them. He'd told her that the dogs' mother had shown up on his property a few years back. She'd promptly given birth to a litter of pups and he'd kept them all. After he told her about the dogs, she wondered if he saw her and Abigail as nothing more than a couple of strays that needed a home. It was a moment of maudlin self-pity, most assuredly, but still, she fretted.

"You think Mr. Bentley is over the moon?" she asked softly. "About... me?"

Harriet smiled gently at her. "Of course, dear."

"I'm not sure what astonishes me more, that he's trying to help my sisters, or that he's fond of me."

Abigail pointed to the window and made some soft, pleading sounds. Grace crossed the room. A deep rumble grew nearer. Soon several cowboys appeared on the road. A herd of cattle trailed behind them with more cowboys flanking the group.

They went to the front porch and watched as the herd thundered past. The dust filled the air but drifted away from the house on a southern breeze.

She searched for Matt and spied him as he rode past, mounted on his chestnut. He fixed his gaze on her and nodded. A curious warmth washed through her, a sweet awareness of the big, scarred, brooding cowboy and the fact that he had his attention focused squarely on her. She smiled and waved as he passed.

I love him...

The thought sent a shock of dismay through her. No, it wasn't possible. She cared for Matt, certainly, but love? How could that be? Surely it was just her foolish heart yearning for what it could never have.

The herd passed, leaving only a few stragglers in its wake. Abigail pointed at them and grumbled, presumably that the fun was over.

Harriet chuckled. "They're taking the cattle to the lower pasture. You could walk through the barnyard, to the hillside and watch them pen the cattle below. Don't stay long, though. It smells like rain. I'm certain we'll get a storm sometime this morning."

"That sounds like an adventure," Grace said.

She bid Harriet good-bye and made her way to the edge of the hillside. Below her were several large pens. The men urged the cattle into the enclosures. Dust swirled. Shouts filled the air. The cattle bawled and jostled each other. Matt looked up at her and once again her heart thudded heavily against her ribs.

In two days, she'd be his.

She would enter the marriage with little to her name, other than the Bentley house. The bank records showed that John's debts were a little greater than his assets. Matt had told her he'd settle the difference.

Thunder rumbled overhead. Grace turned her attention to the threatening sky. Dark clouds hung heavily. A flash of lightning struck the nearby hills.

"Uh-oh," Abigail said softly.

"We have to go home, little one. I'm sorry."

Abigail pouted. Grace turned and began the walk back to the house. A cool gust of wind swept across the barnyard. She grinned at Abigail. "Uh-oh, my love. That's a storm coming. Won't your Uncle Matt be pleased. He's complained about the lack of rain every night." Grace lowered her voice to imitate Matt. "What I wouldn't give for a little rain."

The girl laughed.

As they walked, a light rain fell. Suddenly, the sky opened. The light rain gave way to a heavier downpour. Grace hurried back the way she'd come. After a few steps, the rain turned to hail. Several pieces of hail struck Abigail. The girl cried out with pain and surprise. She clung to Grace, burying her face against Grace's neck.

Grace began to run. The heavy rain soaked her dress. Her skirts were heavy and hindered her pace. The house was too far. She hurried to a nearby barn, hoping to find shelter. She pushed against the door, but it wouldn't budge.

Hail pelted them. Grace felt a sudden desperation that quickly grew to a sense of utter helplessness. She held Abigail tightly, trying to shield the girl from the hail. The barrage hit with such force that she gasped with pain. Each hail stone hit her with increasing force. Abigail shrieked in terror.

Hoofbeats sounded, along with shouts. Matt, mounted on his horse, galloped into the barnyard. He came to a skidding halt, dropped from his saddle and strode to her. Looming over her, he urged her closer to the door well. He positioned himself so that he shielded both her and the child from the hail.

"Turn to me." He set a gloved hand on her shoulder and coaxed her around to face him. "Come on, Gracie. I've got you. Turn to me, sweetheart."

She obeyed instantly, pivoting so she stood with her back to the barn door. She felt him push against her. He set his forearms on either side of her body, sheltering her from the onslaught.

"That's right," he said, next to her ear.

Abigail wept with terror, but slowly she quieted. Her sobs gave way to small wordless pleas. She sank into Grace's embrace. Matt stood close. Grace felt the impact every time the hail hit him. He said nothing, stoically taking the punishment to spare her and Abigail any injury. She rested her head against his chest. He smelled of leather and hard, honest work and a masculine scent that sent a rush of awareness through her. She lifted her gaze and found him looking intently at her.

The crash of thunder and the ferocious rainfall faded from her awareness. She wanted to lift her hand to cup his jaw. Even more absurd, she wanted to press her lips to his. She stared at him, feeling more vulnerable than she'd ever felt in her life.

"Matt..." She breathed his name.

He nodded. His eyes lit with a warm light, one that sparked a heartfelt need deep in her breast. She held her breath. Waited. And wondered if she was the only one who felt the strong need for more.

"It'll be all right, Gracie. I promise. Everything will be all right."

Chapter Seventeen

Matt

The music from the organ filled the small chapel. Friends and neighbors sat in the pews or stood at the back. Matt stood beside Luke and Thomas at the front of the church. A trickle of sweat rolled down his spine. He grimaced and tugged at his collar.

Luke chuckled. “You got butterflies? Cold feet?”

“Neither. I’ve never been more certain of anything in my life.”

Thomas chuckled. “Never thought I’d see the day.”

“You might be next.”

“God willing,” Thomas muttered.

His brother’s smile faded, and Matt knew he was thinking about his first marriage. He’d married young, at barely eighteen. His wife gave birth five months later to a full-term baby. Thomas had confided in his brothers that the boy couldn’t be his. Lorena died a few days later. Thomas raised the boy as his own, of course, naming him Caleb after his own father. Caleb, now ten years old, sat in the first pew, looking bored and uncomfortable.

“That boy needs a mother,” Luke grumbled. “A civilizing influence.”

“Don’t I know it,” Thomas replied.

Matt smiled. Thomas loved his son fiercely, but he was at a loss on how to raise him properly. The boy spent too much time with the ranch hands. He could be polite and well-spoken, Thomas hired tutors to work with him, but out on the range, the boy's manners were worse than those of a mule-skinner. He probably was counting the moments until he could get out of church, out of his fancy clothes and back in the saddle.

Beside Caleb sat Harriet clad in her best dress. She kept a close eye on Caleb, elbowing him when he slouched. She held Abigail on her lap. The girl was enjoying the music. She smiled and waved at him every so often. Her excitement made him smile.

The minister came to the front of the church and shook Matt's hand, and then Matt's brothers' hands. A moment later, a door at the back of the church opened and Grace stepped out. Everyone turned in their seats to see the bride.

Grace walked with Gus. They moved in time with the music. Matt stared. He had tried to imagine this moment so many times, now that it had arrived, he could hardly believe he was really watching Grace walk down the aisle. To him.

Her white dress flowed around her, soft and ethereal. Her veil concealed her face until she drew close. When she was only a few steps away, he could see the nervousness in her eyes. The small bouquet of white flowers shook in her hands.

Unable to look away from her eyes, Matt hardly heard a word the minister said. Luke had to nudge him to say, "I do" and again when it was time to kiss the bride. He lifted the veil, cupped her jaw, lowered and brushed his lips across hers.

There was a polite round of applause.

"You look beautiful, Grace."

"Thank you. So do you." A blush bloomed across her face. "I mean, you look handsome."

Luke came to her side and kissed her gently on the cheek. “Congratulations, Grace. Matt’s a lucky man. We’re all glad you made the trip to Texas.”

Thomas said a few words of congratulations and kissed her cheek too.

The reception was held at Luke and Thomas’s house, under the oak trees. Matt’s brothers had worked tirelessly along with several of his cowboys to make a barbecue. The cook who worked for Luke and Thomas, an older woman from Louisiana, made several Cajun dishes. The men had roasted pork and beef. The party lasted all afternoon, into the evening until the sky filled with stars.

As the night wore on, Matt watched his bride grow more and more tired. She tried to keep a smile on her face while she chatted with guests, but he could see that she faded. People wanted to know about life in Boston, her family, and why on earth a pretty girl like her would come to Texas to marry a stranger. Finally, feeling almost sorry for her, he went to her side and offered to take her home.

“Please,” she said. “Harriet offered to keep Abigail, but I’d rather her be with us.”

“Of course. We’re a family now.”

They made the trip home, guided by the light of a full moon. Abigail seemed almost as tuckered out as Grace. He dropped them at the house and drove the wagon to the barn to unhitch the horses. He rubbed them down and fed them an extra ration of grain.

Walking back to the house, he felt his heart thud in his chest. Grace was in the house, *their* house. Was she waiting for him? Was she nervous? They hadn’t discussed the details of their marriage, but he hoped he didn’t need to convince her they were meant to be together.

Abigail fussed in the nursery. Matt poked his head in. "Do you need help?"

Grace, dressed in a gown and robe, rocked Abigail, trying to soothe her. Matt tried not to let his gaze linger on the way the delicate material looked on her slender frame. Her hair hung past her shoulders, a glorious mass of coppery curls. She was beautiful. And she was his. He swallowed hard, trying to dislodge the tight feeling in his throat.

"I can manage, thank you," she said.

He went to his room, got out of his suit and into a pair of pajamas. The minutes ticked by. He paced, looked out the window, paced some more. Finally, unable to bear another moment without her, he returned to the nursery.

Abigail slept in her crib. Grace dozed in the rocker. He smiled at the sight of the sleeping child and woman. Feeling much like a thief in the night, he crossed the room and picked Grace up.

"Mrs. Bentley," he said quietly. "You're exhausted. Let me tuck you into bed."

She sighed and then laughed softly. "All right, Mr. Bentley."

Gently, he laid her down, helped her out of her robe and after he snuffed out the lamp, he slid into bed. In the space of a minute, it dawned on her where she was. He knew the moment she realized, because he heard the sharp intake of breath.

He remained some distance away from her. Refusing to perch on the edge of his own bed, he settled an arm's length apart. In the semi-darkness he could make out her profile. She lay on her back, staring at the ceiling. Her only movement was the occasional blink.

"This is very... pleasant," she announced, a little too loudly.

He bit back a smile. “It is *pleasant*, isn’t it? This is what we’ll do every night.”

He saw her throat move, heard her struggle to swallow.

“I see. Well, it’s a very big bed isn’t it?”

He rolled to his side, propped his head in his hand. “Is the bed too big, Mrs. Bentley?”

“What? No. Of course it isn’t too big.”

“You could come a little closer.”

The moonlight lit her face with a silvery glow. She pressed her lips together, refusing to answer. He’d seen the obstinate look on her face before. What was it about her stubbornness that made him want to tease her so? He didn’t expect to have his way with his wife on his wedding night, not after such a hasty marriage, but he did yearn for a kiss, even if it was just a peck on the cheek.

“Grace,” he said softly. “Come a little closer. I won’t bite, I promise.”

She turned. “You could come closer too.”

A sweet thrill of victory unfurled inside him. He tried hard not to grin or appear smug. Instead he nodded. “How would it be if we meet in the middle?”

“All right. That sounds equitable.”

She edged closer to him, and he to her. They still weren’t touching, but now they were separated by inches, not feet. “What do you think?” he asked.

“It’s not bad. Unless you think it’s bad. Or awkward.”

“Awkward? Why, this is the most natural thing in the world. A little pillow talk, that’s just what a man wants on his wedding night.”

She sighed and smiled at him.

"We could take this a little further and lie side by side. I might even wrap my arm around you, if that's not objectionable."

"I'm not objecting. I'd like to be an agreeable wife."

"You're a beautiful wife," he said. "And agreeable, so far."

She laughed. "And you're a handsome husband, and agreeable too."

"Shall we meet in the middle?"

She scooted closer and he did as well. The moment her body brushed against his, a wash of warmth flooded his senses. He looped his arm around her waist and let out a deep breath. She flinched and stiffened in his arms.

"Shh... Grace. Stay with me. Everything's going to be all right."

Gradually, she relaxed, sinking into his arms. He held her, marveling at the feel of her so close. Inhaling deeply, he savored her floral scent. As her breathing grew deeper, he smiled. A thousand times, he'd wondered what it would feel like to hold her, but not once did he imagine anything so fine.

Lying next to him, she fit perfectly.

Chapter Eighteen

Grace

Waking in the morning, in the middle of an unfamiliar bed, sent a jolt of shock through Grace's mind. She sat up and looked around. The bed was an enormous four-poster bed. The room was filled with heavy mahogany furnishings that gleamed in the early morning light. The pieces suggested a masculine presence and slowly it dawned on her that she lay in Matt's bed.

Memory of the prior night drifted into her mind. He'd carried her through the house and she'd fallen asleep tucked next to him. In the night, when she stirred, he soothed her with a soft word or two. She shivered, recalling the way his arms felt wrapped around her. The warmth of his embrace and the strength of his hold made her light-headed.

Just then, the door opened. Matt walked in, carrying a cup of tea. He smiled at her and set it on the bedside table. Without a word, he leaned down to plant a kiss on her cheek.

"Mr. Bentley," she murmured. "You brought me tea. In bed?"

"I did. And I came to tell you that Harriet is feeding our daughter breakfast."

She drew a sharp breath. *Our daughter...* "I must have overslept."

"It's all right. You had a big day yesterday."

"So did you."

"I did."

He wore striped pajamas. The blue accented his eyes and she found her gaze drawn to his bare feet. It seemed like such an intimate and domestic thing, to lie in bed in a gown while one's husband strolled around in pajamas.

He went to the wash room. A moment later, he emerged wearing trousers and nothing else. She gasped. Her hand flew to her mouth. He grinned, knowing full well he'd shock her by emerging half-dressed.

"My word," she murmured.

With a smirk he passed the bed, crossing to his armoire. He was powerfully built, with a shoulder span that would fill a doorway. Thick bands of muscles on his arms flexed and rolled as he pulled out a drawer. He turned, giving her a view of his back. Immediately, she saw the mottled bruises.

"Heavens," she said, her voice tight with disbelief. "What happened to you, Matt?"

She threw the covers back and hurried to him.

He turned and frowned. "What is it?"

Taking his hand in hers, she led him to the mirror set over the chest of drawers. "Look at your back."

He turned and looked over his shoulder at his reflection. "Huh."

With that, he returned to his armoire and took out a shirt. He slipped it on and began buttoning the buttons.

He kept his gaze fixed on hers. "That must have happened last night."

She blinked. "When?"

"When I slept with my bride. She has small pointy elbows. All night long, she jabbed and poked me mercilessly."

Recoiling, she put her hand to her throat. Dismay swirled inside her as she tried to recall doing such a thing. All she could remember were the tender things he'd murmured when she woke, and the gentle way he'd held her as she rested next to him.

"No! That's terrible!" she whispered. "Oh, Matt, I feel awful."

He shrugged. "I'll be all right. It doesn't hurt. Much."

"You should have woken me. I could have returned to my bed."

He frowned. "No, I want you next to me. I like the way you feel in my arms. Very much."

She wandered back to the bed. She liked the feel of his arms around her. Last night had been their wedding night and not only had she fallen asleep, she'd spent the night pummeling the poor man. She took a sip of her tea and rubbed her forehead. Turning back to him, thinking she'd apologize for the abuse she'd heaped on him, she found him grinning at her.

"Why are you smiling like that?"

He chuckled. Then he went to the mirror, picked up a comb and combed his hair. He caught her watching him in the reflection. He set the comb down and turned to face her. "Sweetheart, I'm teasing you."

"How so?"

He came to her, cupped her face and kissed her lips. The kiss was soft, but lingering. When he lifted, she saw the laughter in his eyes.

"I got clobbered by the hail, not by you."

She squeezed her eyes shut and shook her head. How could she have been so silly to believe that tale? Opening her eyes, she leveled a look of disapproval directly at his smug expression.

"Wicked man," she murmured. "I was going to insist I spend nights in my own bed."

He shook his head. "No, Grace. Stay with me, always."

She blushed. They hadn't talked about the marriage bed. There were times, over the last few days, she felt certain he'd offered for her merely out of duty. Harriet had suggested he cared for her. After last night she wondered if there was some truth to that. Now, the morning after they'd married, the sweet desire in his eyes sent a thrill through her.

He pulled her into his arms once more. This time, he let the kiss linger. Threading his fingers through her hair, he held her firmly. His lips were warm, his kiss passionate. She felt her knees weaken as she melted into his arms.

When he broke the kiss, he kept her in his embrace. His eyes held hers. They were lit with need and desire and devotion. He stroked her jaw with his thumb. "You've made me so happy, Grace. I can't begin to tell you how much."

Warmth flowed through her body. She nodded. She yearned to tell him a hundred things. How much she loved the feel of his arms around her while she lay next to him. How she prayed she'd be a good wife to him and a good mother to Abigail. The words failed her and the best she could manage was a whispered, "I'm so very glad."

Chapter Nineteen

Matt

Several days after the wedding, Matt received word that Thomas needed to speak to him. Matt left the ranch and rode into town straight to the sheriff's office. He couldn't imagine what the matter was. Caleb sat on the office porch, whittling, a pastime he'd taken a liking to lately. When he saw Matt approach, he got to his feet and waited to take the horse.

"Uncle Matt, my dad caught the rustlers."

Pride shone in Caleb's eyes as he took the reins.

"You don't say. That was quick work on our sheriff's part."

"That's right. My dad's the best sheriff Magnolia's ever had."

"I agree, son." Matt wanted to tousle the boy's hair but stopped himself. Caleb wasn't a child anymore. He wasn't quite a man either, but he was getting old enough to know the difference. "I thank you for taking my horse."

Caleb loosened the cinch and led the horse to the water trough. Matt ascended the steps and entered the sheriff's office, finding his brother bent over a report. He looked up and gave Matt a weary smile.

"Let me guess," Matt said. "Drifters."

A rumble of masculine voices drew his attention. He peered into the cell and to his surprise saw the two Sanders brothers sitting on a bench. They were grimy and scowling and Frank had a blackened eye. Rage surged through Matt's blood. Just the sight of the two men was enough to make him furious. He recalled the way Grace had looked in the alley. The fear that gripped him that day he saw Grace threatened by the Sanders brothers.

Matt gripped the bars and spoke in a lowered tone. "You boys can't find decent work? You got to steal cattle from your neighbors?"

Neither man spoke. Both glared at him, their eyes dark with hate. Soon they'd be gone, hauled to the court in Austin to stand trial. If they were found guilty, they'd hang. It was hard to imagine the town of Magnolia without the Sanders brothers.

All his life he'd worried about run-ins with the outlaw family. He was sure one day they'd take one of his family. Now he didn't need to worry anymore. Not about his brothers. Not about his wife. The thought filled him with deep, abiding satisfaction. Especially the part about Grace. His brothers could fend for themselves, but Grace would be helpless. He curled his hands into tight fists.

Frank smirked, guessing his thoughts.

Matt turned away. Over the next half hour, he recounted the story of how the two brothers cornered Grace. Thomas wrote it down and signed off on the account. The report would be added to the cattle-rustling charges. Thomas was eager to offer the courts every bit of incriminating evidence. After Matt finished giving his statement, Thomas walked him out. They stood on the front steps of the office.

"I should have stayed by her side," Matt said.

"You sure fixed that in a hurry."

"As quickly as I could."

Thomas clapped him on the back. "I didn't think you'd ever marry."

"I didn't intend to."

"Married life treating you well?"

The anger Matt felt earlier began to ebb. He thought about Grace and how much his life had changed in the span of a few weeks. Each evening when he returned home, he felt a wave of overwhelming gratitude for both Grace and Abigail.

"Married life is treating me better than I deserve."

Thomas leaned against a post. "I sent a letter to Faith. I wonder what she'll think of a stranger writing to her."

Matt eyed him with skepticism. "You might need to work on your charm."

"I'm just warming up to the idea of trying this again. It didn't work out too well for me the first time. It's not easy sending for a girl I've never met."

"It's different, Thomas. You're not a kid anymore. You'll know what you're getting into. Besides you need to do this for Caleb. The boy needs a mother."

Thomas nodded. "I know. And I like the idea of having a woman waiting for me at the end of the day. A good woman. Maybe it's not too late for me."

Matt rode home thinking about the woman waiting for him. A rush of warmth filled his chest as he thought of the way she fit perfectly when he held her in his arms. He and Grace hadn't been together as man and wife. Not yet, but the time would come, he was certain. They'd only been married three days. In that time, he'd kissed her, held her and caressed her. He'd held back to ease her into marital relations. Each night he felt her meet his touch with more and more sweet passion.

A few days later, he prepared for bed while Grace tended to Abigail. He decided upon a bath and heated a pot of water on the stove. Her voice, carrying a soft melody, drifted through the house as he carried the hot water upstairs. He filled the tub with hot and cold water until he had just the right temperature. With a groan, he sank into the tub.

At some point during his bath, Grace's singing had stopped. He listened for the sound of her moving around the bedroom. The candle flickered. Shadows danced. A moment later she pushed the door open a few inches.

"Oh! Matt, I'm sorry!"

"You can come in, Gracie." He leaned back in the tub and smiled, imagining her consternation.

She paused and then stepped inside the washroom. The candle lit her face, gilding her lovely features. Her eyes, wide with surprise, shone in the candlelight. Dressed in a white gown, she looked young, innocent, angelic.

"Matt," she whispered.

"Gracie..." He beckoned her with a crook of his finger. "Come, scrub my head. I've always imagined it would be nice to have a wife to help with that."

She bit her lip. "Hmm..."

"Come, sweetheart. I'll lean forward. You can sit down on the floor behind the tub."

She crept across the washroom, her gown rustling as she moved. After she settled behind him, he handed her the soap.

"Your bruises have faded." She worked up a lather and began washing his shoulders.

The touch of her hands on his skin drew a sigh from his lips. "That feels pretty fine, Mrs. Bentley. If you don't mind my saying."

"I'm glad you like it, Mr. Bentley," she replied, her tone playful. "I'd like to be the wife you imagined."

"That so?"

She laughed. "Stop teasing. I'm talking about helping you with your bath."

"Which is precisely what I'm talking about."

"Although one day..." Her words faded as she began to wash his hair.

"Finish what you were going to say." She shifted behind him. He sensed her discomfort as he waited. After another moment passed, he prompted her again. "Go on. Tell me."

"One day I'd like to have children and I wondered if you did, because if you don't, that's fine, because we didn't talk about it before we got married, but I wanted you to know."

Her words came out in a flurry, like she wanted to race through just to be done.

"I'd like that too, even though I worry about the dangers of childbirth. Having a baby here in Texas would be a sight different than having one in Boston."

The soap dripped down his face. He wiped the suds away and glanced over his shoulder. She gazed at him with a fragile look in her eyes. His heart squeezed. He wanted to pull her into his arms and kiss her and comfort her.

"I'm not worried. My mother had easy births, as did her mother before her." She gave him a shy smile. "I come from good, strong stock."

She resumed scrubbing his scalp as if to prove her point. He turned back around.

"All right. That's good to know. Makes me feel a little better. Maybe we'd have a little red-head girl. Pretty like her mama. A sister for Abigail."

"I'd like that too."

He could hear the smile in her voice.

"Ready for your rinse?" she asked.

"Yes, thank you, Grace."

The topic of starting a family had his mind ablaze with a hundred different things. He and Grace would be husband and wife, finally. It had been less than a week since they'd exchanged vows, but in many ways, it felt like a lifetime.

Behind him, Grace got to her feet.

"Close your eyes," she said softly.

A moment later, a blast of ice-cold water cascaded over his head. He gripped the side of the tub and growled. He wiped the water from his face.

"What's the matter?" she whispered.

"You poured the cold water over me. Wrong bucket."

"I'm so sorry." She backed to the door. "My first day on the job didn't go very well."

She stood, pressed against the door, her hand cov ering her mouth.

He narrowed his eyes. "Are you *laughing*?"

A breathless laugh tumbled from her lips. Without responding, she slipped out of the washroom. He got out of the tub, dried off and put on his pajama trousers. He could hear her in the bedroom, trying not to laugh.

He stalked out of the washroom. When she noticed he stood on the other side of the bedroom, she hurried to the bed, scrambled under the covers and yanked them almost over her head.

"Good-night," she said, her words muffled under the blankets.

Circling the bed, he kept his gaze on her, or on the small amount of her that was visible, a few coppery curls that stuck out from under the covers. When he reached the head of the bed, he tugged the covers down.

She yelped and held up her hands to fend him off. She grinned at him, but slowly her smile faded. She swallowed hard. “Don’t hurt me.”

He frowned at her. “I would never hurt you.”

“You seem very big from this angle. And I’ve seen what those fists can do.”

She drew the covers over her face so only her eyes were visible. Her tone was light and mostly teasing, but the words troubled him, more than she probably realized. He stroked her jaw, gently and slowly, relishing the silken feel of her delicate skin.

Her eyes shone as she lowered the covers and gazed at him. “My father,” she said quietly, “had a terrible temper the last few years of his life.”

Realization dawned on him. The small glimmers of fear he saw in her eyes were on account of her father’s ways. Had he been harsh with her and her sisters? Had he hurt them? Matt sensed there was more to the story, but Grace wasn’t ready to tell him the details. Not yet. He felt grateful that she’d shared that small part of herself.

“My hands will only ever protect you.” He spoke gently. “Never to hurt you.” He reached for her hand and wrapped it in his. “Never to hurt our children.”

He lifted her hand to his lips and brushed a kiss across the top. After he turned down the lamp and came to bed, he pulled her into his arms. She sighed happily. He felt her tension give way as she sank into his embrace. The sadness of a moment ago had passed, thankfully. Over time, he’d learn more about his wife.

Nuzzling her neck, he gave her a light nip that made her giggle. “I don’t believe you were a bit sorry about pouring a bucket of cold water on my head, Mrs. Bentley.”

She turned in his arms, making his breath catch in his throat. They'd kissed and held each other every night, but she'd never turned to face him on her own. It was always his coaxing her around so he could kiss her properly.

"How would you like me to give you a Christmas present?" she asked.

"I would like that very much." His voice was rough with desire and he had no idea what he was agreeing to, but it seemed wise to say yes. "It's barely spring, sweetheart. And you're already thinking of Christmas?"

She laughed softly.

"Are you... saying it could be a little one?"

"God willing."

"We'd have to start now then, won't we?"

She nodded. "I believe that's how it works."

He whispered her name, partly in disbelief and partly with heartfelt gladness. Lowering, he claimed her lips with his.

Chapter Twenty

Grace

As the days grew warmer, Grace dressed Abigail in lighter frocks she'd made for the girl. They spent the afternoons indoors reading or playing games. In the evening she'd take Abigail outside to enjoy the cool dusk breezes.

One day, just before dinner, she heard a clang coming from the barn. It sounded again. Grace scooped Abigail into her arms and made her way to the barn. Matt worked in an open area to one side.

Wearing a leather apron, he hammered a piece of red-hot iron. He held it with enormous tongs and bent it around the edge of an anvil. Sparks flew with each strike of the hammer.

"Pretty," Abigail said. She followed this with a frown. "Ouchie."

Grace nodded. "That's right, my clever girl."

At thirteen months, Abigail walked and talked. The child learned things quickly. The walking had quickly turned into running, and she had new words every day.

Matt motioned. As they drew closer, he shoved the piece of steel back into the glowing coals of the forge. Heat waves rippled the air above the forge. The chimney, funneling the smoke, had become thin with time and use. The acrid smell of the fire hung in the air and Grace stopped some distance from the work area, backing away a little when the breeze changed direction.

Matt pulled off his leather gloves, tossed them aside along with his apron, and jogged over to meet them.

"Pew." Abigail shook her head.

He laughed. "Pew – that's right."

Abigail reached for him even though he was covered in a sheen of sweat and smudged with soot.

"No, sweetheart. Look at Daddy's hands."

Abigail made a comical face as she gaped at his dirty hands.

He shoved his hand into his pocket and then held it out, clenched into a fist. "I made something for my little Abigail."

She clapped and grinned. Matt opened his hand to show her his creation, a small piece of iron, a few inches across, hammered into the shape of a duck. The polished metal glinted in the sun. She gasped and tentatively reached out her hand.

"Ducky," she said.

"How sweet." Grace smiled up at him. "It will look so pretty on her shelves."

"I have something for you too."

"Do you?"

"Thomas came by. He said he got his first letter from Faith."

Grace's heart thudded inside her chest. Coaxing air into her lungs, she waited for him to say more.

"He won't share much with me."

"And Faith will share less with me."

Grace tried to push aside her frustration with Hope and Faith. Both sisters had written to say they weren't certain if Texas was safe. Their concern stemmed from John's death from a rattlesnake bite, as well as the story of the rough men in the alley. In retrospect, Grace wished she hadn't said so much. Now she worried that she might have frightened them.

Matt shrugged. "At least Thomas looked happy."

"That's the most we can hope for."

"We'll talk more this evening. Let me finish my work. I have to put the wagon wheel back."

She nodded, optimism blooming inside her. "Harriet says supper is ready when you're done."

"I won't kiss you now." He grinned and held up his grimy hands. "But later, I'll kiss you twice."

She smiled and felt her face warm with emotion. Turning away, she headed back to the house, Abigail on her hip. Unable to resist, she cast a backwards glance over her shoulder and found him watching her, a sweet smile playing on his lips.

That night, after Grace put Abigail to bed, she found Matt in their room. His hair was still damp from his bath. He sprawled across the bed, dozing and clad in pajama trousers. There were times she forgot how tall and muscular her husband was. He lay, bare-chested. Lamplight cast a golden glow across his powerful build. She smiled, coaxed him over to one side of the bed and put out the lamp.

He grumbled, rolled over and pulled her into his arms. She couldn't tell if he was awake or asleep. Impatience stirred inside her. He'd promised to tell her more about her sisters and now he slept. Waiting was almost unbearable. She turned in his arms and pressed her face to his neck. Inhaling, she sighed with pleasure. His masculine scent pleased her in a way she couldn't explain.

His breath hitched. He groaned and ran his hand down her back. "Gracie," he murmured.

"You always smell good. Why is that?"

"Because I only let you get close when I've washed away the grit of the day."

She smiled and nestled closer. "I noticed it early on."

"Mm… really?"

"I did."

"I noticed how you smelled too. Nice. Like flowers…" His voice drifted.

She wondered if he'd fallen asleep, but he pulled her closer and kissed her hair.

"And cake. You smelled like cake too."

"Matt," she said quietly. "I know you're tired, but can you tell me what you wanted to tell me earlier?"

He chuckled and nudged her back to the blankets. He kissed her neck. "For a price."

She threaded her fingers through his hair. The feel of his lips on her sensitive skin made goosebumps wash across her body. Shivering, she sighed with pleasure. "Any price."

He lifted his head. Gazing at her, he stroked her cheek with his calloused thumb. His eyes burned with a fierce light. "I know you're worried about your sisters. If they don't come to Texas to marry, we'll pay for a better boarding house. We'll make sure they're safe and we'll make sure they're well."

She smiled at his words.

"Let me do this, Grace," he said. "Let me make the necessary arrangements either way."

She nodded.

"You trust me?"

"I do."

A rumble of approval vibrated in his chest as he nuzzled her. "Then kiss me, Gracie."

Chapter Twenty-One

Matt

Most towns in the Hill Country had a yearly fair, usually held in the fall. The townspeople of Magnolia long ago decided a single fair wouldn't do. The joke, for many years, had been that they would have *two* annual fairs. A Peach Festival in the spring, and an Apple Festival in the fall.

The morning of the Peach Festival, Matt hitched the buckboard and loaded several baskets of provisions. He stopped by the house. There he helped Grace, Abigail and Harriet aboard the wagon. The three sat in the back on some blankets. Gus arrived, dressed in his Sunday finest, and sat next to Matt.

"Everyone ready?" Matt asked.

The group all agreed they were more than ready to head to town. Matt snapped the reins and the horses pulled the buckboard onto the road. He tugged the brim of his hat down to shield his eyes from the bright morning sun.

Gus gave a wary glance to the passengers in the back of the wagon. "Trouble brewing between the womenfolk?"

Matt frowned. "Not that I heard. Why do you ask?"

"I heard from some of the men that Mrs. Bentley was in the orchard collecting peaches. She had the little one with her. Word is she's made a peach pie for the baking contest."

Matt suppressed a grin. "Does Harriet know?"

Gus recoiled. “Who would be brave enough to ask?”

Both men looked back at the same time. Harriet arched her brow. She gave them a questioning look. Grace held Abigail on her lap and pointed to the cattle grazing on the hillside.

“Doesn’t look like trouble’s brewing,” Matt said.

“That’s the way it works with women,” Gus muttered. “You never know until it’s too late. Oh, you can try asking if they’re bothered by something, but they won’t tell you.” He spoke softly, in a tone that was higher, mimicking a woman’s voice. “I’m fine. Nothing’s wrong.”

Matt grinned. “Is that the way it goes?”

“Trust me. I know these things. Four sisters and twenty years of marriage to Sue-Anne, God rest her soul.”

Matt turned back to Harriet. “Everything all right, Harriet?”

She pursed her lips. “Of course, everything’s all right.”

“You got something for the baking contest?”

Her mouth curved into a satisfied smile. By way of answer, she patted the basket beside her. Then her gaze drifted to Grace. Her smile faded a tiny bit, but she recovered quickly, lifting her chin and giving him a confident look.

Gus shook his head. “That ain’t good. And it gets worse.”

Matt chuckled. “How so?”

“Your brother and I are judges for the baking contest.”

“I agree. That is worse. You wearing comfortable boots?”

“What’s that supposed to mean?”

“You might be walking home.”

“That’s the least of my worries. I was getting to thinking that Harriet might be sweet on me. Now I’m wondering if she was trying to sway my opinion.”

Matt sighed. “The scandal’s going on right under my own nose.”

"That's right. You're too busy thinking about your bride. You walk around with a smile on your face for no reason."

"I don't either."

Gus snorted and then grinned at him.

They arrived at the fair amidst a bustling crowd of neighbors as well as folks who had come from nearby towns. The peach harvest had been the finest in years, and while Matt didn't sell what he grew, there were wagonloads of peaches from other ranches. The ranchers and their families set up under tents, displaying their wares on long rows of tables.

After Matt left the horses and buckboard, he searched the fairgrounds for Grace. She chatted with a few of the ladies who were running the baking contest. In addition to cakes and pies, there were contests for pickles, sausage, jellies and jams.

Abigail squirmed in Grace's arms. Matt smiled to see how excited the girl was by all the hustle and bustle. He came to Grace's side and wordlessly took the girl. Grace gave him a grateful smile and turned back to her conversation with the ladies. Matt wandered the fairgrounds with Abigail. At a game booth, he threw horseshoes, getting three ringers and winning a prize. Abigail's eyes were wide with wonder as she gazed at all the offerings. Finally, she settled on a ragdoll.

She pleaded softly, pointing to the tent.

"All right, Ducky," he said.

Abigail chuckled at his pet name for her.

Inside the tent, he found Luke and Gus talking in earnest. Both men wore looks of concern. Luke raked his fingers through his hair and shook his head.

"How did I get roped into this?" he asked.

Abigail waved the doll for Luke to see. He smiled at her. "That's a nice little dolly, Abs. Don't you look pretty in your yellow dress. You want to help Uncle Luke judge the baking contest?"

Matt laughed. "You leave the innocent children out of it."

Suddenly sharp words rang out. Matt turned to find the source of the outburst. At the far end of the tent, Harriet spoke angrily to a man and woman. Matt recognized him as a rancher from a neighboring town, a bitter and small-minded man. Grace stood nearby, pale and shaken. Matt strode across the tent.

"Uh-oh," Abigail murmured, her eyes wide.

"You have some nerve talking to a young woman like that." Harriet seethed, her face florid with anger. "A girl who's come all the way from Boston to become part of the Bentley family."

The man and woman, looking properly chastened, stared at Matt.

Harriet jerked her thumb at the couple. "Mr. Jones was telling Grace that she's hardly the grieving widow, marrying so soon after John's death. I say it's none of anyone's concern and we're blessed to have her here. Especially little Abigail."

Matt had never seen Harriet so angered, but his main concern was Grace. He moved to her side, tucking her under his arm. She sank against him. Before he could say something to defend his wife, she spoke.

"I never met John," she said quietly, addressing the couple. "He passed away while I traveled to Texas."

The man thinned his lips. "Still. It don't seem proper. The man's barely cold in his grave and his widow's dallying with the brother." He sneered at Matt. "You couldn't wait to get your hands on the pretty little-"

"Take Abigail," Matt said to Grace. "Leave the tent."

Grace took Abigail into her arms and hurried away. Matt stalked towards the man, backing him against a corner table.

He outsized him considerably and it would have been no trouble to teach him manners, but he didn't want to be responsible for any violence at the fair. Not with all the families around.

He spoke quietly. "Grace is my wife. I won't tolerate anyone speaking to her disrespectfully. Leave now. Go home. If you ever address my wife again, I'll hear about it, and you'll be very sorry."

The man smirked. "I've heard about you, the youngest Bentley brother. I guess it's true. You're as ugly on the inside as you are on the outside."

Matt set his hand on the man's shoulder. The man recoiled. He probably thought he was safe here amid a throng of merrymakers. Matt squeezed the man's shoulder with a silent warning.

"I am, in fact, uglier on the inside than I am on the outside. And if you ever disrespect my wife again, you'll be spitting teeth."

Chapter Twenty-Two

Grace

Finding the bedroom empty, Grace wandered downstairs. The house was dark with no sign of Matt. She pushed the front door open and peered out. He sat on the porch swing. She went to him and when she drew near, he took her hand to coax her down to his lap.

She looped her arms around his neck. "Aren't we the scandalous pair, Mr. Bentley."

He growled softly and wrapped her in his embrace. "Troublemakers. I wish they wouldn't come to Magnolia. I'm sorry he said that to you."

"I'm not bothered by it. I expected some people might not welcome a newcomer."

"He won't be back. When Luke heard what happened, he followed him back to his wagon and gave him a piece of his mind. The fellow took off in his wagon while the onlookers cheered."

She buried her face against his neck. "This is going to be talked about for years to come, won't it?"

"I don't think so." He kissed the top of her head. "People in Magnolia are decent folk. They wouldn't abide slander."

"I'm sorry to be the cause of any commotion."

"Hush. You caused nothing."

She sighed and closed her eyes, relishing the feel of his strong arms around her. Whenever he held her, she always felt comforted and protected. Never had she imagined she'd find such happiness in her husband's arms. Making the trip to Texas had been a matter of necessity. Although it ended with the tragedy of John's death, she found herself a contented wife. More than contented, really.

"Abigail loves her little doll," she said. "She's taken it to bed with her and fell asleep holding it."

"Her first fair. Her eyes were big as plums taking in all the sights."

"It was my first fair too." She looked up at him. "And to think I came home with a blue ribbon."

He smiled. "Gus fretted that he'd be in trouble with either you or Harriet."

"Harriet's quite proud of her baking. You should have seen her face when I told her I wanted to make my mother's peach cake."

"I can imagine."

"All week, she teased me mercilessly. First, she said the peaches I'd picked were sour. Then she claimed the stove wasn't heating properly. Finally, she flat-out threatened to put a heaping tablespoon of salt in my batter when I wasn't looking. She's fierce, that Harriet."

"Yet you won, despite it all."

"She claimed she was joking about the salt. That she'd never do that considering it was my first baking contest."

"So come time for the next fair, she might sabotage your entry?"

"I am a little worried, frankly. But she still ended up with a blue ribbon too."

"How so?"

"Luke said the baking contest was going to be divided into a cake category and a pie category."

Matt chuckled. "That was some quick thinking."

"It was."

He laughed and tightened his hold on her. "I could hold you like this all night."

"Scandalous," she murmured.

"You're falling asleep?"

"Mm..."

"Let me carry my blue-ribbon bride to bed. I think she's tuckered out."

When they got to the top of the stairs, a muffled cry came from Abigail's room. Matt set Grace down and moved to the door to listen. Grace came to his side and set her hand on the door. He put his finger to his lips and motioned for her to stay at the door.

She listened as Matt went into the room.

"What's the matter, Ducky?" The deep timbre of his voice made her smile. "Your doll fell out of your bed?"

"Yes." Abigail sniffed.

"All right let's see if I can find her in the dark."

A moment passed, then another. Grace heard him rummaging around, patting the floor and muttering. There was a bang. Matt grumbled a few indistinct words of complaint.

Abigail offered her sympathy. "Ouchie..."

"Ouchie. That's right, Abigail. Here, I found her under your crib. Tuck her in beside you so she doesn't get lonesome."

"Mkay."

"Goodnight, darlin', sweet dreams."

A moment later Matt appeared in the hallway and shut the door softly behind himself. Together, they walked to their room, both ready for rest. They slipped beneath the covers. Matt settled beside her and sighed contentedly. “I might need to see if I can buy about a dozen of those little dolls.” He rubbed his head. “Else I’ll be crawling around in the dark every night.”

Chapter Twenty-Three

Matt

Over the next two weeks, Matt was gone long days, riding the range to check the herds. Most of the cows were getting ready to calve, and the new mothers often struggled the first time around. He and his two brothers always did this chore together, along with Gus.

The old cowboy probably knew more about cattle than anyone. Gus had worked for Matt's father. His father liked to say that Gus could recognize a cow he'd seen ten years prior as a calf. Neither Matt nor his brothers knew if that was accurate or just a tall tale, but Matt would put his money on that being exactly right.

As tired as he was when he came home each evening, he was grateful for Gus's help. Without the old-timer's expertise, they'd probably lose plenty of calves along with their mamas.

The two of them rode home on the last night of range-riding. The trail turned the direction of the barnyard, winding through the prickly mesquite. Dusk settled across the rugged land and the setting sun cast the barn in silhouette.

"So Gus, is Harriet still sweet on you, or was that all just for show so her peach pie would get your vote?"

Gus scrubbed his hand down his face. "I dunno. She's still sweet on me, I guess."

"We going to have a wedding one of these days? Maybe a few little Guses and Harriets?"

"Ha! That would be a miracle. The two of us are too old for any of that."

Matt grinned. "I figured. But you could still have a few happy years together."

"I'd like that," Gus muttered. "I just need to convince Harriet that we'd be a good match. She says I'm cantankerous."

Matt chuckled. "Really? Mrs. Pot, I'd like to introduce you to Mr. Kettle."

"Exactly. I'm no more cantankerous than she is. But then she's got a sister's that's not well. She goes on about Clem and how she's needed. I got to thinking I need her too, but that might be too forward."

Matt's gelding pricked his ears, looking towards a grove of oaks. Wild turkeys foraged on the ground around the trees. When they saw the horses, they made a fuss, took flight and settled amidst the oak branches.

"Gobblers are going to roost for the night," Gus said. "Can't say it's a bad idea."

Even though Matt had been up since before dawn, he approached the house with a light heart. The anticipation of seeing Grace and Abigail always made his chest warm with happiness. After they returned to the barn, he and Gus untacked and fed their horses. Once their work was done, Matt wished him a good night and went directly to the house.

The aroma of dinner perfumed the air. His stomach grumbled, but he wanted to see Grace first. He heard her in the nursery, rocking the baby. Instead of disturbing them, he ate the dinner that Harriet had left. After, he took a bath and scrubbed what felt like ten pounds of grit from his skin.

Usually, Grace would come sit with him while he bathed. They'd talk about the day while she washed his back.

Tonight, he found her lying in their bed. He came to her side and took in her wan appearance. Reaching for his hand, she gave him a tired smile.

"Are you sick, Gracie?"

"It comes and goes."

He lowered to the bed. His heart crashed against his chest as he watched her lower her hand to her mid-section. She held it there, not moving. He set his hand over hers.

"Are you expecting, sweetheart?"

His tone was gruff. Why that was so, he couldn't say. He felt happy. Thrilled. Mostly. Part of him felt a deep, icy dread flowing through his veins. He managed to coax his lips into a hopeful smile as he waited.

"Maybe," she said softly. "We've been married almost two months now."

He nodded. "Right."

Her mouth curved into a smile. "It's a baby, Mr. Bentley. It's something that happens every day."

"I know." He got to his feet and went to the window. "What do you need? Help with Abigail?"

"No." Her voice trembled.

He turned to find her staring at him with tear-filled eyes. Moving quickly, he came to the bed and settled next to her. As the tears spilled down her cheeks, he gathered her in his arms and soothed her with soft words. "I'm sorry."

With his eyes closed, he chided himself for his callous response to her news.

"Aren't you happy?" she whispered.

"I am. So happy. I love you so much. I want this. It's just a bit of a surprise."

She swatted his shoulder.

"It's not a surprise," he hastened to add. "It's more of a shock. That's all."

He stroked her hair and smiled down at her. Her lids lowered, and he studied the fringe of lashes and the tears that clung to them. Guilt twisted inside him. She'd offered him the happiest news he could hope for and he'd given her a cold response. He was happy, certainly, but he worried too. Grace was delicate. Fragile. He'd just found the woman he loved with all his heart. How could he bear the idea of her facing anything dangerous?

Chapter Twenty-Four

Matt

The blades of the wooden windmill lay scattered across the ground. Back in January, a winter storm had made short work of the windmill Matt's grandfather erected forty years ago. All that remained was splintered wood. With his boot, he nudged the debris.

"I remember a time when wooden mills were all you saw," Gus said as he knelt beside the wreckage.

Luke shook his head and grimaced at Matt. "A sight easier to work with."

"Steel is better," Matt said. He gestured to the bed of the wagon where a new mill lay, glinting in the morning sun. "A little paint and grease every so often, it'll last a century."

"You knocked that out in a hurry," Luke said.

"I worked on it in the evenings," Matt said.

His brother gave him an inquisitive look. Matt ignored him and went to the mule team hitched to the buckboard. He didn't want to talk about his evening work with Luke or anyone for that matter. Since Grace had told him she was expecting, she'd suffered from fatigue and stomach upset. Every time he saw her, she seemed to be feeling worse. His thoughts always drifted to what she might suffer during childbirth.

He berated himself for not waiting longer to consummate the marriage. There had been a time when he intended to simply offer a marriage of convenience. If he'd stayed true to that idea, Grace wouldn't be suffering from morning sickness, or facing the perils of childbirth.

He could hardly look at her pale countenance without wrenching guilt. Soon it became easier to seek solace hammering the steel blades of the new windmill. He spent the evenings working off his restlessness. He didn't like to be away from her, especially if she needed help with Abigail, but she never wanted to trouble him for anything.

He took hold of the mule's harness and backed the wagon to the base of the derrick. It would take some luck, a little finesse and a whole lot of brute strength to hoist the mill. He'd worked out the plan with Luke the night before and now it was time to put the design into action.

Over the course of the morning, he and Luke tied the pulley system and tested the ropes. They climbed up and down the old windmill, tying the ropes at four-foot intervals. Gus stood on the ground surveying the work, feeding them lengths of rope as they progressed.

When the rigging was complete, the three men stopped work to drink from their water canteens. They rested in the shade. Before long, Harriet appeared, trudging up the path, a basket over one arm.

She waved. "I've brought lunch. Roast beef sandwiches on bread fresh out of the oven."

Gus took the basket from her. "Did Mrs. Bentley make the bread?"

The old-timer missed the slight narrow of Harriet's eyes.

"I made the bread," Harriet said with a sniff. "I hope everyone likes it."

"It smells wonderful," Luke said.

"Mrs. Bentley only bakes on Sundays," Harriet added. "The day I leave mid-day to visit Clem."

"The other day she brought me a piece of her lemon cake and I have to say..." Gus's words trailed off as he caught on to Harriet's displeasure.

Harriet pursed her lips. "You have to say *what*?"

Gus glanced at his two companions, seeking an ally. Both Luke and Matt gave him blank looks. Gus cleared his throat and shifted from foot to foot.

"I have to say that I've never had lemon cake before." He took off his hat and rubbed his forehead before proceeding. "It was very, very, er... lemony."

Harriet grumbled and turned her attention to the picnic. "Speaking of lemons, I made lemonade for you menfolk. Little Abigail even squeezed some of the lemons, bless her. She's quite the little helper in the kitchen. Mostly she just played with the lemons, but I was glad for the company."

Matt wondered how much time Abigail had spent in the kitchen that morning. Grace must not have felt well. That would be the only reason Harriet would have been minding Abigail. Tension coiled in his muscles. He pictured her face, pale and taut from queasiness.

There were nights where he had terrible dreams of Grace suffering. The dreams were always the same and he could almost hear her cries. He'd awaken in a cold sweat. He'd lie in bed, watching her as she slept and as he wrestled his fear of losing her.

He married her to protect her. He married her because he was in love with her. The possibility that he'd put her in harm's way was more than he could bear. The idea of having children had thrilled him. It still did, but dread lurked in the shadows of his mind.

Despite the warm day a chill came over him. “How’s Gracie?” he asked.

“Still having a little trouble keeping food down. Nothing to worry about, though. She’s looking a mite thin, I’ll admit, but she can tolerate my potato soup. I keep it bland with just a little salt. I had a batch simmering all morning. I’ll give her a little for her lunch when I get back.”

Harriet handed each man a sandwich wrapped in a dish linen. They ate while she poured lemonade into mugs. As she handed Matt his, she gave him a pointed look.

“You needn’t worry, Mr. Bentley,” she said. “My mother always said it’s a good sign when a woman feels poorly the first few months. Sign of a healthy baby.”

“You don’t say?” Gus marveled.

Harriet kept her gaze fixed on Matt. “She’ll be fine. You mark my words.”

Matt took a swallow of his drink and nodded.

“Women are not fragile,” Harriet said. “Especially not Grace.”

Matt was certain that wasn’t true, but he wouldn’t bother arguing.

Harriet went on. “No need to treat her like she’s made of spun glass.”

Luke and Gus smiled at the woman’s mild reproach. They watched Matt for his response. Everyone knew that disagreeing with Harriet was reckless.

“Yes, ma’am,” he drawled. “If you say so.”

She beamed and patted his arm. He ate his sandwich, wishing that someone would change the subject to anything other than Grace’s condition. He poured himself more lemonade. “Lunch is good, Harriet. Thank you.”

“Especially the bread,” Gus added.

Harriet waved a dismissive hand. "Ha! Sweet-talker. I'll be on my way then. Shall I leave the basket with you men? There's more of everything."

"We'll set it on the wagon when we're done," Luke said.

She turned to Matt. "I'll expect you for dinner? Or will you be working late again. Banging around on things in the smithy..."

"I won't be home for supper tonight," Matt said. "This work will take us till dark and later. But tomorrow night, I'll be home."

"All right," she said, grudgingly. "She'll be looking for you around dusk, though. Just like she does every night."

"Tell her I'll be home when I'm done." He caught the look of mild reproach she gave him. "And I won't work late in the barn."

With that she gave him a smile. "I will. Good day, gentlemen." She dusted off her hands, muttered a few words about her work being done, and set off for home.

Chapter Twenty-Five

Grace

Usually the queasiness got better in the evening, but not tonight. Harriet had cautioned her about having seconds of the roast chicken, but Grace couldn't resist the woman's cooking, and lately, when she was hungry, she was ravenous. Now the meal troubled her. She lay back on the chesterfield and closed her eyes.

Abigail, in her sweet innocent way, seemed to know just when a wave of nausea hit. Grace tried to hide the fact that she felt poorly from the child, but at times it was impossible. Abigail set her hand on hers and murmured softly.

With a sigh, Grace opened her eyes. "What did you say, darling?"

"Mama..."

Grace sat up and gathered the girl in her arms. "Why, Abigail, my little angel."

Abigail snuggled in her arms and let Grace lift her to her lap. Harriet came to the parlor to look in on them. She crossed the room and bent over to gaze at Abigail.

"What did I just hear?" A smile lit her face.

"This clever girl just said a very special word."

Harriet chuckled, and gathering which word Grace meant, she pointed at her. "Who's that, dear?"

Abigail, suddenly shy, smiled up at Harriet but said nothing.

"Go on," Harriet urged. "Who is that?"

"Mama."

Harriet set her hand to her heart and drew a sharp breath. "That's right, Abigail. You *are* a clever girl." She straightened. "It's been so long since I've had little ones around. I hadn't realized how much I missed it. I just had the one. Susannah. She's grown up now, a teacher in Houston. I don't think she'll ever marry. She says if she does, she'll send for me, but I can't imagine leaving the Bentley family. Especially now."

Grace shook her head. "I can't imagine you going away, Harriet. How would we manage? Besides, my sisters might be coming, and I've told them all about you."

"Two more O'Brian girls," she mused. "I hardly dare to hope."

It was late, close to bedtime. Abigail rubbed her eyes. She already had her bath and wore her gown.

"She's tired," Harriet said softly. "Shall I carry her upstairs for you?"

"I can manage."

Harriet shook her head and gave her a disapproving look. "If I can't take the girl, I'll carry the warm water to your bath."

"I'm sure."

"I won't take no for an answer. Go on, now. I'll have the bath ready by the time the little one's drifting off to sleep."

"Yes, ma'am," Grace replied dutifully. There was no way to argue with Harriet. Gus had warned Grace when she first arrived. He muttered something about how Harriet would get the bit in her mouth. Grace hadn't known what that meant, but over time, she understood the meaning perfectly.

Harriet regarded the Bentley boys as her charges. She never said as much, but it was clear to Grace. Harriet had appointed herself substitute mother to Luke, Thomas and Matt, and, by extension, to her and Abigail as well.

Grace knew Harriet missed John. She wasn't sure how close Harriet was to the eldest Bentley. Perhaps not as close as she was to the others. Grace suspected that was because John had a wife, while the other brothers were bachelors for so long. Harriet longed to have them married off almost as much as Grace did.

Grace carried Abigail upstairs to the nursery. She made sure she was dry and sat down to rock her to sleep. Harriet had mentioned once or twice that Grace was spoiling the girl by rocking her to sleep, but Grace explained the baby hadn't known much tenderness in her young life. Grace fully intended to spoil her a little. Harriet hadn't argued the point. If anything, she'd agreed with a quick nod. She sniffed a little, hurried away and didn't mention the subject again.

Abigail settled immediately, but Grace lingered in the nursery. Every moment with Abigail was a moment she didn't have to spend alone, waiting for Matt to return. Since she'd told him about the baby, he'd grown more and more distant.

At first, she told herself he was a hard worker. She was fortunate he provided well for them. As the weeks passed, she felt her loneliness more keenly. The evenings had become the hardest part of the day. Each night she fell asleep alone in their bed. Sometime in the night, he'd settle beside her and by morning he'd be gone.

When she'd imagined starting a family with Matt, she thought it would bring them closer, that it would make their love grow. That was not the case. Something about the pregnancy drove a wedge between them. She pictured his face and felt a deep well of yearning in her breast.

Reluctantly, she put Abigail to bed. She said a prayer for the girl and tucked her in, and as she wandered to her room, she recalled that Harriet had promised a bath. By now the water would, at best, be barely warm. She pushed the bedroom door open and gasped to find Matt lying in the bed. He sprawled across the covers, his hair wet from the bath, clad in a pair of loose trousers.

"Oh," she said with surprise, her heart filling with warmth. "You're home."

"I am. I've been home for a while."

"I'm so glad to see you."

He rose from the bed and drew her to the candlelit washroom. "I used the water Harriet left for you, but I brought up more. Can I help you?"

Her face warmed. "I can manage."

He took a letter from the side table and waved it in the air. "From your sister, Faith."

She held out her hand, but he shook his head, a smile playing on his lips. "After your bath."

With a slight huff, she took a quick bath. Her heart raced as she dried off and slipped into her gown. She'd gotten only one letter from Faith, and that had been before Thomas had started writing. She hoped and prayed that the letter contained good news. Would Thomas offer for her and if he did, would Faith make the trip? How much easier it would be to convince Hope to come to Texas if Faith were already here.

She got into bed and lay next to Matt as she read the letter. Her sister wrote about the goings on in Boston and nothing about Thomas until the end. In the final paragraph, she explained that Thomas had offered for her and she'd decided to accept.

Grace read the last few lines aloud. "I've decided that I'd very much like to be a rancher's wife."

"That rascal didn't tell me a word," Matt grumbled.

Tears of happiness spilled from her eyes. She wiped them away, feeling foolish for her emotional display. Her condition seemed to play havoc with her feelings. Several times a day, she'd tear up over some small thing that other times she would hardly notice. Matt smiled at her and kissed her tenderly.

"I wonder if she knows that Thomas works as the sheriff for Magnolia," Grace murmured. "She didn't say a word..."

"I don't know. But she's coming. That's the important thing. One down," he said with a chuckle. "And one to go."

Chapter Twenty-Six

Matt

To celebrate the good news of Faith coming to Magnolia, Matt offered to take Grace to the Bentley family's swimming hole. He and his brothers had enjoyed many afternoons swimming in the crystal-clear waters. Her face lit with happiness when he told her of his idea over breakfast.

"Just as soon as you're well enough," he said.

"I'm feeling fine today."

Matt watched as Grace coaxed Abigail into eating a biscuit. "There's a shallow spot that's shady. You and Abigail could wade in the water."

"I could sew swim clothes for her and for myself. Next summer, when I'm not expecting, I can take her in the water."

"Swim clothes, huh?" Matt smiled, unable to resist teasing her. "I've never seen a lady in swim clothes. Probably because I've never been swimming with a lady. My brothers and I used to run around..."

Grace blushed. "Matt, stop."

"Naked as a needle."

"Shh, Abigail, don't listen."

They resolved to go later that afternoon and have a picnic by the water. Harriet fussed about Grace overtaxing herself but packed a basket anyway. Matt sent word to Thomas and Luke about the outing. Mid-afternoon, he packed the buckboard with blankets and the picnic. He helped Grace up with Abigail and they set off.

The spring lay in a valley that ran between Matt's and Luke's homes. The buckboard rumbled along the dry creek bed. Groves of pecan trees lined the banks and encircled the spring.

"My grandfather planted these trees forty years ago," Matt said. "In the late fall they'll produce."

"We don't have pecan trees like these in the north."

"They grow well because this area floods every so often. Pecans are thirsty trees."

"It's beautiful down here. We could have walked."

"Harriet would have had my hide."

He stopped the wagon beside the spring. While she spread the blankets he held Abigail. They walked along the bank. Minnows darted into the depths. At first, Abigail gazed in wonderment. Then she pointed at the fish, laughing in delight each time she spied one.

Thomas and Caleb rode up a short time later. Thomas's son wasted no time kicking off his boots, tossing his shirt aside and diving off the bank.

Abigail watched and uttered a soft, "Uh-oh."

"Brings back memories," Thomas said.

Grace pointed to a small cabin tucked between two towering pecan trees. "What's that?"

Thomas and Matt both grinned.

"Come," Matt said. "We'll show you."

They made their way along a path. Thomas pushed the door open and showed Grace the inside of the cabin. It had been a good long while since they'd stepped foot in the cabin, but everything was just as Matt remembered.

"Our father made this cabin for us," Matt said. "The four of us spent many a summer night down here."

Bunk beds lined the wall, four of them. Matt's gaze drifted to the lower bunk to the left of the fireplace. His heart sank as he thought of John. He exchanged a look with Thomas, but neither spoke.

"What a sweet little cabin," Grace said. She walked the length of the room to the fireplace and looked around admiringly.

"Caleb would love to come down here and spend the night like we did," Thomas said. "I won't let him. Not by himself."

Grace nodded. "It might be a little risky for a boy to come alone."

Thomas sighed. "I ought to bring him myself."

"Maybe," Grace said with a shy smile, "you can come with Faith."

Thomas colored. "It wasn't easy to convince her to come. She seemed to have some misgivings about the Bentley men."

Matt frowned. "Why is that?"

Thomas went to the window and looked out. "A letter arrived from you, telling Grace not to come, but she'd already left. Apparently, you mentioned something about mail-ordered brides not being a very good idea."

Grace lifted her hand to hide her laughter. "The poor man is stuck with one now."

Before Matt could reply, his brother went on. "And then she got a letter from Grace, saying that Matt Bentley was an insufferable bully."

Matt snorted.

Grace's smile vanished, and she looked sheepish. She bit her lip and looked almost apologetic. "He was, Thomas. You have to believe me."

"I do. I promise I do. But I'm not sure if she's coming to marry me or to make sure that you're doing all right."

Grace winced. "I don't think that's true. I've written more letters telling her how wonderful life is here in Magnolia."

Luke and a dripping Caleb appeared in the doorway. "I wondered where everyone was."

The cabin felt cramped with the six of them inside.

"We were showing Grace the cabin," Matt said. "And Thomas is explaining how he had to sweet talk Faith into accepting his offer."

Luke snorted and rolled his eyes. "All I hear come out of that man's mouth is Faith-this, Faith-that."

Grace gave him a pointed look and cleared her throat.

"I'm sorry, Grace," Luke said. "But I can't stay on in that house if Thomas is going to be carrying on like that. She might be here in less than a month."

"You can move in here." Matt tried to keep from grinning. "It would be kind of cozy."

"Very funny." Luke scowled and leaned over to look at one of the bunks. "I'm not even sure the beds are long enough for an adult."

"I believe I'm the owner of John's house," Grace said.

Luke straightened. "I'd thought of that. And there's no one living there right now."

"If you marry my other sister, you may have it."

Luke shook his head and left the cabin, muttering under his breath.

Matt and Thomas laughed. Grace gave them a look, mocking wide-eyed innocence. They wandered back to the spring and sat along the water's edge. They ate a light dinner as the sun began to set. Since the evening was warm, Grace took off Abigail's shoes and let Caleb take her into the shallow part of the spring. The water came a little past her ankles. She laughed and smiled, her antics making the others join in.

Later that night, after Abigail was asleep in her crib, Grace came to the bedroom and slipped into bed next to him. Matt dozed but found himself drawn to her, needing to feel her near. Without thinking he pulled her close and drifted off to sleep.

“Grace,” he whispered. “You’re mine. Always.”

Chapter Twenty-Seven

Grace

The next two weeks passed by more slowly than Grace believed possible. Every day she hoped for a letter from her sisters, or news from Thomas, but there was no word from any of them. Thomas said he was waiting too. He'd sent money for Faith's trip, offered to send for Hope, but the days passed without a reply.

The good news was that Grace's morning sickness began to fade. In truth, she'd suffered from morning sickness throughout the day, not just in the mornings. As she began to feel better, her appetite returned, a development which pleased Harriet even more than it did Matt. Harriet threw herself into cooking with a renewed vigor.

One day, the ranch received news that shocked everyone.

Grace had just put Abigail down for a nap when she heard several riders arrive in the barnyard. The horse's hoofbeats told of men in a hurry and she wondered if anything was the matter. She went downstairs to the kitchen and found Harriet looking out the window.

"Thomas and Luke rode up like the devil himself chased them," she said.

Grace came to her side and watched as Matt spoke to his brothers. Gus wandered over and listened to the three men discuss something that must have been quite dire. All of them frowned, except for Matt who wore a dark scowl.

When he turned his attention to the house, his eyes quickly found her at the window, and he stared at her. Her blood ran cold to see the raw fury in his eyes. She'd never seen such rage, certainly not in her husband's eyes.

Even when he'd knocked the men in the alley down, he hadn't had that feral look about him. Slowly, he turned away and spoke a few more minutes to his brothers. She stood rooted to the spot, unable to look away. Her throat tightened. She swayed a little and set her hand on the window frame.

"Gracie?" Harriet asked. "Are you having a spell?"

"It's nothing."

"You're feeling poorly? Your stomach?"

Grace shook her head. "I'm fine. I've never seen Matt look quite so furious. It's a little unsettling."

"I can't imagine what they're talking about. I pride myself on minding my own concern."

"You do?"

Harriet knit her brows.

"I mean, of course you do," Grace hastened to add.

Harriet unlatched the window and slowly inched her fingers to the handle. "It's not really eavesdropping if they see us standing here, is it?"

"Um..."

"Shh... don't talk. I can't hear."

"I should come too," Matt said.

Grace drew a sharp breath and looked at Harriet with alarm. "What?"

Harriet lifted her finger to her lips.

Thomas spoke next. "You're a family man now. You need to stay home. Luke and I can take care of it. I'll send Caleb to stay with you."

Matt nodded. "Of course. Harriet dotes on the boy."

Harriet scoffed.

"That's mighty kind of her," Thomas said. "He needs a woman's touch."

"He needs a good smack on the head," Harriet muttered. "That's what the little hellion needs."

"We'd best be going," Thomas said.

The men spoke a few minutes more before riding off.

Harriet shut the window. "I'd say Thomas and Luke are chasing some outlaw. That's my guess."

"Dear lord," Grace whispered. "Thomas has offered for Faith. What if..."

Harriet patted her arm. "Now dear, there's no need to worry about things that aren't in our hands. Don't get yourself in a tizzy over a string of what-ifs."

A few moments later, the front door opened, and footsteps sounded in the hallway. Grace left the kitchen and went to Matt's study. There she found him fastening a gun belt to his waist. The sight of the weapon made her recoil.

"You're leaving," she said.

She'd heard him say he wasn't but couldn't imagine why else he would need a gun. Her gaze drifted to the weapon. The cold steel glinted. The leather was tooled, ornate and worn.

"I'm not leaving. Thomas and Luke are. The men who cornered you in the alley, the Sanders... they escaped from jail."

Grace let out a soft huff of surprise. She hadn't thought of the men in weeks. The notion that they'd ridden free unnerved her. Her hand drifted to her stomach. "Heavens."

"It will be fine, Grace. I'm just being cautious in case they show up. They made some threats."

Grace bit her lip, her attention returning to the weapon. "What will you do if they come here?"

His gaze darkened. The hard expression returned to his eyes. He closed the distance between them and cupped her shoulders. She flinched. For the first time since she'd known Matt, she wanted to retreat from him, to escape his touch.

"If I see those men on my property, I'll kill them."

A cry of dismay fell from her lips. She'd never seen this side of Matt, never even imagined it. She shook her head, trying to push the violent words out of her mind.

"I'll kill anyone who comes around intending to cause trouble. Them or anyone else."

She swallowed hard.

His gaze softened. "You, Abigail, our baby, you're all mine to protect. Understand?"

"Yes," she breathed.

"Until we get word that the men have been caught, I don't want you to go anywhere on the ranch without me or Gus."

"Of course."

Chapter Twenty-Eight

Matt

Caleb arrived just before dinner, riding the gelding Matt had given him for his last birthday. The horse's coat gleamed, and the tack looked freshly oiled. The rider, on the other hand, looked like he hadn't seen a bathtub in an age. His clothes were stained with grass and dirt. His pants hung a few inches too short. Clearly the boy took good care of his horse, but he spent no such time on himself.

Still atop his horse, Caleb spoke.

"Uncle Matt, did you hear the Sanders men escaped? Dad's gone to look for them with Uncle Luke. I get to stay with you."

"Heard all about it. Happy to have you here."

The boy's grin lit his face. He dismounted and patted his horse. "My dad says that Rusty's the best horse he's ever known."

"I can tell you're taking mighty fine care of him. Warms my heart."

"Watch this, Uncle Matt." The boy turned to the horse and held up his hand. "Stay, Rusty."

Matt watched as the boy walked halfway across the barnyard. He turned to face his horse, but for a moment didn't say a word. The horse, ears pricked forward, waited attentively.

Caleb motioned with his hand. "Come, Rusty."

The horse walked several paces towards the boy.

"Stop," Caleb commanded when the horse was still a few paces away.

The horse stopped.

"I'll be," Matt said. "I never seen anything like that. Can you make him sit? Roll over? Play dead?"

Caleb laughed and shook his head. "Not yet. Come, Rusty."

The horse closed the distance between them. Caleb took the reins and turned to face him. "Take a bow, Rusty."

To Matt's astonishment, the horse dipped his head almost to the ground and lifted it back up.

"Why, that's about the best bunch of tricks I've ever seen, Caleb."

"Yes, sir, and you should see how he works cattle. I can cut steers faster than any of the Bentley cowboys when I'm riding Rusty. He's the smartest horse around."

"He's got a good owner. Don't forget that part. How about we untack him and give him some supper? I've got a stall with fresh straw for him."

Caleb followed Matt into the barn, chattering about how he'd show Faith how to ride when she came, and he'd show her the swimming hole, and a dozen other things.

"You excited about her coming?"

"Yes, sir. I sure am. I just wish my father wanted a passel of kids. He says one is plenty, and that I've already given him a few gray hairs. Which isn't true. He doesn't have any gray hair."

Matt undid the cinch and took the saddle off the horse. He wondered if Thomas might change his mind about children. Matt had fallen hard for Grace. He hoped Thomas might follow the same path, but he knew that, deep down, Thomas had a distrustful nature, especially when it came to women and matters of the heart.

"Besides, Faith might not like Daddy after all," Caleb added. "I read her letters. She wrote that she's coming despite her reservations." Caleb spoke in a high-pitched voice, setting his hands on his hips to mimic Grace's sister. "I love my sister and feel the need to make sure she is well. If all is indeed well, we can consider proceeding."

Matt chuckled but stopped himself when he saw Caleb's amusement fade away.

"What if she comes and doesn't stay?" Caleb asked. "What if she doesn't like me?"

The boy's words made Matt's heart sink. Caleb, like Abigail, never had a mama, only four ornery uncles. He said a silent prayer that Faith would look kindly on the boy, and on Thomas too. The wistful look in Caleb's eyes left him unsure what to say.

Caleb patted his horse. "Anyway, she'll like Rusty, don't you think?"

"Of course, she will. How could she not like such a smart horse?"

Caleb slipped the bridle from the horse, told him to come along and led him to his stall. He shut the door and brushed off his hands. "I'm starving. All I've had today was flapjacks and an apple."

"We'll have to see what Harriet rustled up for us."

Caleb eyed the gun at his side and gave him a winning smile.

"Yes, Caleb, you can shoot the pistol. But not this evening. We have to warn the ladies before we start shooting tin cans. Your Aunt Grace is in the family way. We don't want to frighten her or anyone else."

Matt looked the horse over. “Did you bring a satchel? Where are your fresh clothes?”

Caleb wrinkled his nose. “Fresh clothes?”

“Never mind. We’ll make do.”

They left the barn and walked to the house. An evening breeze rustled through the leaves. Swallowtails swooped, darting through the air, catching mosquitoes. The dogs lazed on the porch but roused when they saw Caleb. The boy had a way with animals, that much was certain.

“Maybe I’ll get a mail-order bride one day,” Caleb mused. “How old do I need to be to get one?”

Matt bit back a smile. “I’m not sure about that. You’d need a home and a way to provide for her.”

“I know that. I want to get married as young as possible. I want plenty of kids. A dozen.”

“That would be something. Check back with me in a few years and I might have a better answer.”

The dogs trotted down to meet them. They circled around the boy, tails wagging. He bent to tousle their fur and say a few words to each.

“When we get inside, you go wash up. Say hello to Harriet and Aunt Grace. If they say anything about a bath, tell them your Uncle Matt said you could wait till after dinner.”

The boy grumbled a few indistinct words but followed them with, “Yes sir.”

They parted ways in the front hallway. Matt went into his study, unfastened his gun belt and listened as Caleb’s footsteps faded. Ever since this morning when Thomas and Luke had told him about the escaped men, he’d been wary. His light-hearted conversation with Caleb had eased his worried mind. Caleb’s yearning for a family tugged at his heart. Caleb was a good boy. Hopefully, when Faith came, she would see that in him.

He heard the kitchen door open. An instant later there was a shriek. Harriet let out a sharp yelp of dismay. Matt chuckled. He put the gun in its case.

"Merciful heavens," Harriet cried out. "Who is this filthy little ragamuffin coming into my kitchen?"

"Aw, Harriet," Caleb's muffled response came. "You know it's me. Your favorite ragamuffin."

Chapter Twenty-Nine

Grace

By the time Caleb had spent his second night, Grace was certain the boy was Abigail's favorite person in the world. Her face lit when he entered the room and his antics never failed to make her laugh. Often his display would serve as entertainment for the girl and a means to tease Harriet.

One morning, several days after he'd arrived, Harriet brought a basket of muffins to the table where Grace and Abigail sat with Caleb. Matt hadn't come to the table yet. Harriet frowned at Caleb, noting his uncombed hair. Deliberately setting the basket out of his reach, she chided him.

"You need to be presentable when you come to my breakfast table, young man. Wash up and do something about that mop."

When she left, Caleb pretended to be a cat. He made a show of licking his paws, mewing and rubbing his face and head. He knew Abigail was fascinated with the barn cats, and his display would earn him a smile from the girl. Sure enough, she giggled at him, delighted at his charade.

Grace couldn't keep from laughing at the boy.

Harriet returned with a platter of scrambled eggs and bacon. After she set it down, she turned back to the kitchen, giving Caleb a light smack on his head. She bustled back to the kitchen. Caleb pretended to be injured and tumbled from his chair. He landed on the floor with a crash and an exaggerated groan.

Abigail's peal of laughter made Matt smile as he came to the table.

"Someone's going to be sent from the table with an empty belly," Harriet called from the kitchen.

Caleb jumped to his feet and hurried to do her bidding.

Matt kissed Grace and sat at the head of the table. Over breakfast they talked a little about the bit of news they'd had of Luke and Thomas. The word was the two had joined with a group of lawmen. They searched the smaller towns as well as the outlying areas.

The subject filled Grace with dread, but she tried not to let on. She couldn't imagine how worried Caleb was about his uncle and especially his father. He seemed stoic as he talked with Matt about prior manhunts. Even a little proud.

When breakfast was over, Caleb helped clear the dishes.

"I don't think he's discussed his work with Faith," Grace said to Matt.

Matt looked thoughtful. "Maybe he didn't want to scare her off."

"It seems very dangerous."

"Not for my father," Caleb said as he gathered the plates. "He always finds his man. Sometimes he just strings them up right there in the desert, so they can't escape again."

Grace felt the blood rush from her face. "What?"

Caleb began to explain, but Matt stopped him. "That's enough."

Abigail began to fuss. Grace wiped her face and hands, took her from her chair and held her on her lap. Neither she nor Matt spoke. She could see he didn't want to discuss the subject further, but the more Grace wondered about the truth of Caleb's words the more she fretted. Yesterday, Matt said he'd be willing to kill the men if they ventured onto Bentley property. That was equally upsetting to her.

Later that morning, after becoming increasingly distraught, she resolved to put the matter out of her mind. She found Caleb in the garden, helping Harriet pick okra. They watered the plants with water they'd pumped from the well.

"When he's done with his chores, send him in. I'd like to measure him for some trousers and a few shirts."

Harriet nodded and shooed him inside. "He can go. We've finished."

Caleb grimaced, but did as he was told. He trudged inside, kicked off his boots and followed Grace through the house.

"I have a little sewing room beside your Uncle Matt's study. Abigail likes to play with her doll by the window. I made her a little nursery for her baby."

"I don't think I need new clothes, Aunt Grace. I'm fine."

"Is that so? What about when my sister comes? She and Thomas will exchange vows. Are you going to wear trousers that show your bare ankles?"

He sighed. "No, ma'am. I'll wear the same trousers I wore when you and Uncle Matt got married."

"That's what I mean. Your pants are all too short." She smiled as she took his measurements. "With your handsome dark hair, I'll have a nice array of colors that will look fine on you. Why, you'll be quite the dandy."

"Luke will give me a hard time about that."

"He'll need something nice to wear too. The suit he wore to our wedding looked like it's seen better days and he can't come to church in dusty cowboy clothes."

When she finished the last of her measurements, Caleb asked if he could leave. The moment the permission was out of her mouth he hurried away. Despite her worries about Thomas and Matt and the men who roamed the hills of Magnolia, she had to chuckle. A moment later, Harriet appeared in the doorway, red-faced from gardening.

“Warms my heart that you’re being so kind to the boy,” Harriet said. “The boy needs a mother in the worst way. You think your sister will care for him?”

Grace took the slip of paper with the measurements and set it on a little side table. She glanced at Abigail. The girl sat in a pool of sunshine, her locks catching the golden rays. She was so intent on playing, she hardly glanced up at Grace.

Grace turned back to Harriet. “Don’t worry about Faith. She’s one of the kindest people I know. She’s sweet and beautiful and...”

Her words drifted off as she thought of her two sisters.

“Without any faults,” Harriet mused. “Spoken like a loving sister.”

Grace smiled. Usually the subject of Faith and Hope was bittersweet. She loved them. She enjoyed writing to them and receiving their letters in return. Now that there was a real possibility that Faith would come, she was filled with eagerness. Once she had Faith settled, she’d work doubly hard to get Hope to come.

Since the wedding, Matt had offered to send for them, but they’d been reluctant, claiming they didn’t want his charity. Hope had been the most stubborn. They also voiced concerns about the dangers of life in Texas. Somehow, Thomas had convinced Faith to put her worries aside and journey to the Bentley Ranch.

"Faith is a good person," Grace said. "If anything, she's sometimes a little too trusting. She'll give a stranger the coat off her back. I do hope Thomas appreciates her sweet nature and cherishes her."

Harriet went to the window and gazed down at Abigail playing with her doll. "Too trusting. They'll be a good fit, then. Thomas doesn't trust anybody, except his brothers. He trusts them. And you, of course. He wouldn't send for Faith if he didn't esteem you."

Grace drew a heavy sigh. "I've never played matchmaker before."

Harriet came to her and patted her hands. "It will be fine, dear. Don't fret."

"I'll be glad when the outlaws have been captured, the men have returned, and things have settled. Then I can look forward to my sister coming."

It was true. She felt the worry keenly, like a weight on her shoulders. The notion that dangerous men lurked the countryside troubled her. But there was more. She also fretted about the new side of Matt and Thomas. She'd never imagined they might be capable of violence. Her hand drifted to her stomach and she imagined the tiny life inside.

"Sometimes..." she said softly.

"What's that?" Harriet asked.

"Sometimes it all seems so precarious."

Harriet nodded. "It's all in God's hands, dear. We can rest assured of that."

Chapter Thirty

Matt

Word of Thomas's injury came at daybreak.

Somehow, Matt sensed things had gone awry for his brothers and risen early. He whispered a few words to Grace and left the house. Once out of the house, he went straight to the barn, hoping to find Gus with a pot of coffee. Instead, he found his foreman with a deputy from the town of Pecos, a sleepy settlement not far from Magnolia.

"Your brothers were ambushed, just outside of town. It was straight up an act of revenge," the young man said, his jaw tight from gritting his teeth. "Thomas will be all right. The doc's taking a ball out of his shoulder now."

"I saddled your horse," Gus said. "I'm riding with you."

Matt shook his head. "I won't leave the women here alone."

The deputy took off his hat and raked his fingers through his hair. He was young, earnest, one of Thomas's newest hires. He glanced at the house and back at Matt. "I can stay here, sir."

The fellow looked pale and flustered. Thomas's injury might be the first time he'd seen a fellow lawman get hurt. He probably wanted to avoid a grisly scene with the surgeon.

Matt gritted his teeth, wondering what he'd find in town. He nodded. "I'd be much obliged."

They set off, riding as fast as the terrain would allow. With good time, they made it to Magnolia in less than a half hour.

As they rode into town, Matt felt a wave of gratitude for the good weather. It hadn't rained in a long while, which made life on the ranch difficult most of the time, but today, needing to ride fast through creek beds and turned soil, he was glad everything was completely dry.

The men went to the doctor's office first. Doc Phillips was the only doctor in town, the same man who'd tended to John. Matt prayed that Thomas would be a better patient than John. He also said a quick prayer that the two outlaws had been caught. Or better yet, killed.

They arrived at the small building where the surgeon conducted most of his business, a clapboard cottage behind the doctor's home. Two deputies from the town of Pecos waited outside. They came forward to take Gus and Matt's horses.

"How is he?" Matt asked.

"He's coming to," one of the men said with a wry smile. "Just heard him cuss at the doctor."

Matt left Gus outside, hurried into the cottage and almost collided with Luke. Luke leaned on the desk of Doc Phillip's nurse, clearly flirting with the girl. Matt scowled at his younger brother.

"Can I assume that Thomas is still alive if you're out here visiting?"

The nurse blushed. "Yes, sir. He's doing much better, sir."

Luke grinned. "He's not pushing up daisies just yet."

Thomas's voice came from the back of the small house. A groan, and then a few words Matt assumed were directed at the doctor, none of them particularly flattering. Matt arched a brow and glanced at the nurse.

"He's been talking the whole time the doctor worked on his shoulder," the nurse said. "It's been... colorful."

Matt felt the tension in his neck loosen. The circumstances weren't dire, at least, which was a tremendous relief. He and his brothers were still mourning John. The family didn't need another funeral.

Matt turned to Luke. "How did Thomas get shot?"

"Around midnight, we were riding near Pecos. We'd gotten word that the men were holed up in an abandoned prospector's cabin. The plan was to surround the cabin, me, Thomas and two other men, but we got separated from the others. The cabin was empty. We were about to ride into Pecos but got ambushed. Thomas took a bullet to the shoulder."

"The two Sanders men?"

"Jed got away. I got Frank."

Matt narrowed his eyes. "Meaning?"

Luke glanced at the nurse and then back at Matt. He cleared his throat. "Meaning, he won't cause anyone any more grief, ever again."

The nurse paled and hurried into the back.

"How bad is Thomas's shoulder?"

Luke shrugged. "I'm sure it hurts like a son of a gun, but the bullet didn't hit bone. Doc thinks it went straight through."

A shout came from the back, followed by a string of curse words.

Luke sighed. "Poor Penelope, she's getting an earful. Doc might be looking for a new nurse all over again."

"She one of your sweethearts, is she?" Matt asked.

"I'm just being friendly, is all."

Matt snorted and took a few steps towards the back room. "Think I can go look in on him?"

"You can try. Doc ran me off. Said he could only deal with one Bentley brother at a time."

Matt waited, passing the time by pacing the floor. It troubled him that Jed still roamed free. He told Gus to return to the ranch. He wanted both Gus and the deputy on hand in case there proved to be any problems.

Finally, the doctor emerged from the back, looking weary. “Thomas is going to be fine. The bullet passed through his shoulder and left a very clean wound. I’d like to keep him here till evening. You can send a buckboard for him then and take him home. Feed him a light supper. He might not feel like eating, but he’ll need to keep up his strength.”

Matt held out his hand to shake the doctor’s. “Thank you, sir.”

The doctor nodded. “He’s lucky.”

Matt turned, put his hat on and paused at the door. “Better lucky than smart.”

Chapter Thirty-One

Grace

The news of Thomas's injury came as a shock to Grace. She was grateful when Matt brought his brother to the house so that she and Harriet could tend to him. Thomas's injury, as terrible as it was, gave her hope that he might give up his work as a sheriff. Over the days following Thomas's injury, the topic caused a few short-lived debates between Grace and Matt.

Thomas sought to reassure her that the job was important, but rarely dangerous.

"Frank got lucky," he told her one evening over dinner. "That's all."

"I know it's important work," she said. "But you have a son to care for, a bride on the way. Once Faith arrives, I'm certain you'll want to spend as much time with her as possible, courting and wooing her."

Thomas sat at the other end of the table, his arm in a sling, a wry grin playing on his lips. "Court her?"

"What's that mean?" Caleb asked.

Grace smiled at the boy. That morning she'd finished two new shirts and a pair of trousers. He wore them to the dinner table and looked so nice that he even got a compliment from Harriet. Something about him turning into a handsome young man. He'd blushed furiously but smiled too.

"When you court a lady, you take her on walks in the moonlight," Thomas told his son. "You say nice things about her eyes and such."

Caleb snickered. He resumed eating the roast chicken Harriet had prepared. Grace could tell from his expression that he didn't believe a word his father said. She and Matt exchanged a smile.

"I'm sorry I haven't done that, Mrs. Bentley," Matt said, setting his hand on hers. "I promise to start right away."

"I'll hold you to it, Mr. Bentley."

Thomas tried to cut his chicken, which proved difficult with just one hand. Caleb jumped to his feet, took his father's knife and fork and cut the chicken for him. Thomas sighed and muttered under his breath a few words about being tired of having a useless arm.

Abigail watched Caleb with interest, and when the boy was done, she called him to attend to her food. It was already cut, of course, but she always liked attention from him. "Calep," she called to him. "Calep."

Caleb grinned at the way she said his name. Gallantly and with fanfare, he went to her side. He cut a few pieces of chicken for her, making the already small pieces even smaller. She smiled with satisfaction and resumed eating, her eyes sparkling with happiness. She smiled up at Grace, her sweet face making Grace's heart melt.

"You love that Caleb, don't you, darling?"

Abigail laughed.

"It's fun having a little kid around," Caleb said. "I can't wait till Faith and Dad have kids. I'd like a little brother. I think he should be called Simon."

Matt chuckled. "First we need to get Faith to Texas. And then Thomas has to court her."

“Faith doesn’t know you’re the sheriff of Magnolia, does she?” Grace asked.

The table quieted. She’d been eager to ask the question for some time. She’d held back because part of her felt like she was meddling. On the other hand, she didn’t want Faith to arrive to find surprises. She herself had gotten off the train and been greeted with the shocking news of John’s death.

Thomas gave her a thoughtful look. “That’s a fair question. In the past, my work hasn’t taken me away from the ranch very often. I took the job, not because I wanted to. Magnolia had a run of corrupt lawmen.”

His words left her without response. She turned to Matt, giving him a questioning look.

“It’s true,” Matt said. “It’s one of the reasons we don’t have too many womenfolk in Magnolia. For some years the town had a reputation for lawlessness. They said Magnolia was the Dodge City of Texas.”

Grace shook her head, not comprehending his reference to Dodge City.

“Dodge City is famous for gunfighters, saloons and...” his words drifted. “Other unsavory activities.”

“What’s unsavory mean?” Caleb asked, his eyes lighting with curiosity.

Grace half-expected Thomas to silence the boy, or ignore the question, but he did neither. He thought for a moment before going on.

“The subject’s not fit for young men, but one of the unsavory things I can tell you about, son, is the gambling. Cowboys come to town with their wages and play cards. Sometimes they win a little, but often they get taken by cardsharps. They get cheated out of their honest pay.”

Caleb looked thoughtful. “That’s like stealing.”

"It *is* stealing."

Grace watched as Thomas spoke to Caleb. Over the last few days, she'd had the chance to see him with his son. When Caleb arrived at the house, disheveled and wearing ragged, too-small clothing, she'd wondered what kind of father Thomas was. Now she saw that while Thomas might not pay attention to regular baths, he was attentive and loving.

Caleb had surprised her too. A few times she'd mentioned a book or verse, and each time Caleb knew the story and could recite the entire verse. He told her that his father hired tutors to come to the house and give him lessons. Thomas ignored pant cuffs that were too short, but he cared for the boy in many important ways. Although she wished he'd give up being a sheriff, she admired her brother-in-law, and hoped fervently that Faith would as well.

Chapter Thirty-Two

Matt

That night, Matt resolved to take his wife for the moonlight stroll that they'd discussed over dinner. It would do them good. Ever since the outlaws had escaped from jail, she'd eyed him with a wariness he'd never seen before. She hated the gun and the threat of violence. At times he wondered if she might be a little afraid of him.

He waited for her to put Abigail to bed, a strange nervousness humming inside him. He couldn't understand it, but the feeling reminded him of the awkwardness he'd felt around members of the gentler sex. The unease plagued him before he met Grace and had all but disappeared since then. For some reason, it had returned that evening.

The walk in the moonlight would have to be done on the porch. He wouldn't take his wife away from the house for a moonlit walk until Jed Sanders had been found. There was word that he'd been shot in Marfa, but the news was unconfirmed.

When she came into the bedroom she looked at him with surprise. "I thought I'd find you readying for bed."

"I wanted to take my wife for a moonlit stroll. A short one."

"A short one?"

"Yes, just on the porch."

He half-expected her to laugh, but instead her gaze softened. Her eyes shone. A sweet smile curved her lips. "Thank you," she said softly.

He moved closer to her and cupped her shoulders. "I should have done this a long time ago. From the beginning."

She blushed. He was struck by her loveliness just as he was anytime he drew near her. Grace was so beautiful, sometimes it stole his breath.

"Ready?" he asked, his voice gruff.

"I am."

He offered his arm. She stared for a moment, not moving. "Gracie," he said gently. "This is the part where you let me escort you outside into the moonlight."

"Yes," she said, hastily. "Of course."

"If you're trying to make me feel bad, it's working."

They went down the stairs together. She shook her head. "I'm not. I promise."

As they passed the sitting room, they heard Thomas and Caleb talking quietly. From the doorway, he glimpsed them sitting on the chesterfield, heads bent over a checkers game. Thomas had always been an attentive father, but in the three days since he'd had a bullet go through his shoulder, he'd doted on Caleb even more.

He led Grace outside. The three ranch dogs sprawled across the porch. They lifted their heads and peered at him, thumping their tails with mild confusion as if wondering why people were coming onto the porch at this hour.

"Git," Matt ordered.

Their tails stilled, and they stared in bewilderment.

"Off the porch," he said, more sternly this time. The dogs got up, slowly, their expressions woe-begotten. They ambled off the porch, all three looking over their shoulders as they left.

Grace laughed softly. "They're wondering if you mean it."

"I do," he grumbled. "Hard enough to stroll on a porch without having to jump over sleeping dogs."

The porch wrapped halfway around the house. Roses lined the railing, offering their perfume and scenting the night air. A breeze ruffled the plants. When Matt and Grace walked to the end of the porch, they stopped and looked out into the darkness. Matt pointed to the horizon. "See the silvery light? The moon's going to rise any minute now. Gus told me it would be full tonight."

She turned to face him. "Did you tell him you were planning on courting your wife?"

He could hear the smile in her voice. Wrapping his arm around her waist, he drew her closer. He brushed his lips against her cheek. "I didn't, sassy girl. He was sitting with about ten of my cowboys. If they knew I was trying to be romantic, they'd never let me forget it."

She leaned into him and he tightened his hold on her, letting his hand drift across her narrow waist. She was as slim as she'd been the day he first laid eyes on her. He wondered when she might begin to show. He loved the idea of her carrying their baby... that is, he loved the idea when it didn't terrify him.

"I suppose one day," he said softly. "I'll touch you and feel the baby move, right?"

"Yes, Harriet says that happens around four months."

"And you're how far along?"

"Three months, I think."

Happiness warmed him, filling him with contentment. "Sweetheart..."

He lifted her chin to kiss her. Shadows darkened this corner of the porch. He thought she might be shy and resist, but she submitted to his kiss. Her lips were soft and warm, her kiss was gladly given, making him wonder why he'd waited so long to take his wife out for a moonlit stroll.

"Do you intend to steal kisses or court me?" she teased.

He bent to kiss the tender skin along her neck. She laughed and squirmed when he reached the spot on her neck that was especially ticklish. He smiled to hear the sound.

"Why can't it be both?" he asked.

"I suppose it can be both. I'm not aware of the rules, but I think you're also supposed to say fine things about my eyes."

"Right. Your eyes. Thomas did mention that. Let me think on it." He tried to think of something charming and heartfelt. Darn that Thomas. Thomas probably knew several things that a man might say to a lady that would show appreciation for her eyes.

He looked around, scanning the night sky. In the moments he'd kissed Grace, the moon had crested the horizon. It hung in the sky, immense and the color of amber.

"Your eyes," he began, "are round and beautiful like the moon. Like two moons."

"Two moons?"

"Yes, like two moons."

Well, that didn't sound quite right. The pretty words weren't easy to come by. He drew a deep sigh and thought about courting and wooing. Now it seemed like a terrible idea. Why the need for this tricky stuff? Instead of trying to explain further, he turned her, coaxing her around so she could see the moonrise. "See. Not bad, right?"

"Ah, yes," she mused.

He could hear the teasing lilt in her voice.

"I hope my moon-eyes aren't orange," she said. "I might need to see the doctor."

"Grace," he muttered. "You're not making this easy on me."

She laughed softly. "No, I suppose I'm not."

Stepping behind her, he wrapped his arms around her and held her close. Lowering, he whispered in her ear. "Your eyes are *not* orange. They're perfect. Just like the rest of you, my sweet, sassy wife."

That sounded a little better, he thought, and maybe she considered it an improvement as well because, for once, she didn't have a smart reply. She stroked his arm, leaned back and rested her head against his chest. They stood in silence, arms entwined, letting the quiet peaceful night surround them. When she sighed softly, he thought about her delicate condition. His protective instinct took over. She was tired. She was working harder than she should with the needs of Abigail and Caleb. Without a word, he clasped her hand in his and quietly led her inside.

Chapter Thirty-Three

Grace

The next time Harriet made a trip into Magnolia, Grace asked if she could come along. Both Gus and Matt went, as did Caleb. Gus drove the wagon and Matt rode beside him, scanning the horizon. He wore his gun belt as he did anytime he left the house.

Thomas felt certain Jed Sanders was dead. Two reports from Travis County corroborated that he'd been shot in a saloon. While neither witness could say how badly Jed had been hurt, Thomas was certain the wound would kill him. Plus, he reasoned out loud, if Jed had survived being shot, he wouldn't come back to Magnolia. Not without his brother, Frank.

Despite his brother's reassurances, Matt insisted on carrying a weapon. He also insisted on accompanying Harriet and Grace to the shops.

"What do you want to buy?" Matt asked as they walked down the wooden planks of the sidewalk. She carried Abigail on her hip. He set his hand on her lower back, a protective gesture that always warmed her heart. She reveled in his gentle touch.

"I'd like to buy myself some material to make my husband a few shirts."

He smiled at her. "You do so much, Grace. For me and for others."

"I enjoy it immensely. I love caring for you and Abigail. And Caleb too."

Caleb walked ahead, keeping pace with Harriet. He was telling her a story of the fish he'd caught in the creek near his house, deliberately exaggerating its size. Harriet laughed at his outrageous claims. He was a good-hearted boy, eager to please. Well, mostly eager to please. Grace noticed he delighted in vexing Harriet when he got the chance.

Thomas had gone back to the sheriff's office to check on reports, but he'd spent most of his time doing ranch work. Although he'd returned to his home, Caleb had stayed behind, living with Matt and Grace. No one bothered discussing his presence or questioned why he remained. Grace secretly hoped he'd stay on for a good, long while.

They entered the mercantile. Caleb wandered to the knife cabinet and Matt followed him while the ladies looked over buttons and material. Harriet eyed the goods with a furrowed brow. She ran her palms over the fabric, turned the buttons over to examine the details.

Abigail wanted to get down and walk. Grace wasn't so sure about that idea. She let her down but held her hand firmly as they negotiated the narrow and cluttered aisles. The mercantile was so different from shops in Boston. Crates were stacked precariously. Boxes were strewn along shelves. New merchandise was constantly being brought in from wagons in the back. Just as quickly, it would be purchased by a rancher or cowboy.

The first time Grace had come to the mercantile, the owner's niece had waited on her. A soft-spoken beauty named Emily. Grace recalled how the girl seemed to fear her uncle.

She also recalled how out of place the girl looked, attending to the rugged, cowboys.

She glimpsed Emily, standing at the back of the store, her face pinched with distress. A man spoke to her in a gruff tone. His words sounded urgent, although Grace couldn't make them out. Dressed in cowboy garb, he held himself with a certain authority that struck Grace as familiar. When he turned, she saw that the man speaking to Emily was Baron Calhoun.

Perhaps she'd picked up Harriet's habit of eavesdropping, for Grace wanted nothing more than to hear the exchange between the handsome banker and the shy shop girl with the fragile smile. Emily looked away, averting her gaze from Mr. Calhoun's fierce expression. In the shadowed light, Grace saw plainly that a dark bruise marred the girl's lovely features.

Grace took a sharp breath. Try as she might, she couldn't tear her gaze from the girl's face, or the way Mr. Calhoun looked at her. He looked like an animal ready to spring. Bile burned in Grace's throat.

Emily turned away from Mr. Calhoun, retreating through a door. He followed. The door closed behind him.

Grace's heart raced. She stared at the closed door, praying that the girl would come to no harm. Mr. Calhoun seemed a good man. In truth, it was the uncle that worried Grace.

On the way home, she asked Harriet about the imposing man.

"Baron Calhoun is a decent man," Harriet said. "He convinced Thomas to become the town's sheriff. I hear he's the toast of Houston. I seem to recall he was courting Governor Stanton's daughter. If they marry, he'll be richer than Croesus which should suit him fine. Why do you ask, dear?"

Grace gathered Abigail closer in her arms. The child yawned sleepily and closed her eyes as she snuggled against Grace. Grace sighed. "I saw him talking to the shop girl."

Harriet made a face. "She's a pretty little thing, but mark my words, Baron Calhoun prefers young ladies with pedigrees and rich fathers."

Chapter Thirty-Four

Matt

That evening, as they finished supper, word came from the bunkhouse of two cowboys fighting. Matt could hardly believe what he was hearing. One of his men stood on the porch, disheveled and wide-eyed, telling him that a feud between two of the new hires had come to a head.

Matt tore down to the bunkhouse and stormed inside. Broken furniture littered the floor. Gus lay slumped against the wall. Two men circled each other amid the chaos. They were new men, cowboys he'd hired for the drive north.

The bigger man, Hines, landed a punch that toppled his opponent. And that should have been the end of the brawl. Instead of calling it a day, Hines began kicking the other while he lay on the floor. The sound of his boots hitting the man enraged Matt. Kicking a man while he was down was fighting dirty. No two ways about it.

"Hines!" he roared.

The cowboy ignored him. Matt grabbed him by the collar and hauled him back. Hines sneered and lunged, his fist missing Matt's chin by an inch. Matt hadn't intended to fight the man but had no choice. He made quick work of it, landing two quick punches that connected with Hines's jaw. The man staggered back.

He swayed on his feet as he eyed Matt.

The two men faced each other. Matt waited. Hines held up his hands in a gesture of defeat.

"Pack your things. I want you off my ranch by nightfall."

"I didn't start it," Hines said.

"I don't care."

"Gus is always playing favorites."

"Is that why you hit him?"

Hines nodded. "A man gets tired of pulling the short straw."

"You better not let me see your face again, or I'll take care of you the same way I take care of rustlers."

Hines curled his lip but didn't argue. He smirked as Gus stirred and groaned. He turned and kicked the foreman. Matt charged across the room, snarling as he grabbed Hines by the shirt. Fisting his collar, he slammed him against the wall and delivered a series of blows to Hines. He didn't stop until the man collapsed at his feet.

"Hitch the wagon," he ordered. "This man's going to jail."

Matt left Gus in Harriet's care. Surprisingly, his only injuries were a goose egg on the back of his head and a black eye. After, Matt took Hines to Magnolia and left him with Thomas's deputy. Hines was just coming to when he left. He gave Matt a baleful look but said nothing.

Matt got home just before full dark. Gus lay in his cabin, eating a piece of cake Harriet had brought him. Harriet assured Matt that Gus would be fine and to go on to the house.

Grace waited for him at the top of the stairs. Dressed in her gown, she was pale and trembling. He went to her, folding her into his arms. Instead of softening like she usually did, she held herself back as if she didn't want his touch.

"What is it?" he asked.

She took his hand in hers and it was then that she saw the bleeding knuckles.

"I got into a little scrape is all," he said.

Nodding, she turned away and went to the bedroom. He followed.

"Caleb told me everything," she said quietly.

"Sometimes these things happen."

"I understand."

"Do you?"

She swallowed. "Yes."

He moved closer, needing to touch her, to reassure her that everything would be fine. He'd make sure of it. But she stepped away, retreating.

"Gracie...?"

She shook her head. "I'm tired, that's all."

He left her, went to the washroom and washed himself. She'd been afraid of him. He'd seen it clearly in her eyes. She'd never looked at him that way before. When he returned to the bedroom, he found she'd put out the lamp and lay with her back to him, probably feigning sleep.

Chapter Thirty-Five

Grace

Over the next few days, Grace had her hands full. Harriet spent several hours a day tending to Gus, who seemed to revel in the attention his injuries earned him. So, it was with relief when Grace found her in the kitchen making dinner.

"I haven't seen Mr. Bentley all afternoon, have you?" Harriet asked.

"I haven't either," Grace replied.

Her heart thudded heavily against her ribs. She and Matt hadn't spoken much since the fight in the cowboy's bunkhouse. She'd avoided him, unable to explain her fears. He probably thought she was a hysterical city girl. Or maybe he thought her heightened emotions were due to her pregnancy. Either way, she'd found being near him made her fretful.

During dinner, she'd find her gaze drifting to his hands. They were big and strong and had only ever touched her gently, but the idea of him beating another man frightened her. She'd seen him beat the two Sanders men. She remembered vividly how his rage that day darkened his features.

"He's in the barn," Caleb said, snatching an apple as he passed through the kitchen. "He said he's not coming for dinner."

"He's not?" Grace's throat tightened. She wandered to the window. Dark storm clouds hung low in the sky. Thunder rumbled around the house. "He never misses dinner."

"He must be tending the mare. She's set to foal," Harriet said. "Gus told me all about it. I'll send you a plate, Mrs. Bentley, if you want to take him a bite."

Grace eyed Harriet. At times the woman called her by her first name and other times she addressed her as Mrs. Bentley. Grace wondered if she knew there was some uneasiness between her and Matt.

"Abigail's napping," she said. "I shouldn't leave her."

Harriet pursed her lips. "I suppose I can mind the girl."

Another blast of thunder shook, rattling the windowpanes.

Normally Harriet fussed over her. Now she wanted to send her out in a thunderstorm. Grace narrowed her eyes, trying to discern the woman's intent, but Harriet gave nothing away. She merely served ham, fried potatoes and beans onto a plate. She hummed as she worked, covering the plate with a linen napkin.

Handing Grace the plate, she practically shoved her out the back door. A few drops of rain fell on her head. She lifted her skirts a few inches, so she could make haste and cross the barnyard as the occasional raindrop turned into a steady downpour. A few steps from the barn door, it opened, and Matt appeared, smiling at her.

"Hello, Mrs. Bentley. Nice day for a walk."

"Harriet wanted to send dinner." She stepped inside and handed him the plate. "And she elected me as the delivery girl."

He shut the door behind her.

"I was going to go straight back, in case Abigail woke from her nap."

"Harriet can take care of her," he said.

Grace ran her hand across her brow to wipe the raindrops away. He brought her his jacket and draped it around her shoulders. Sitting on a wooden grain box, he tossed aside the napkin and surveyed the food.

"Looks good. Thank you."

She moved closer, stopping a few paces from him. "What are you doing in the barn?"

"Keeping an eye on a mare. She's going to have a foal in the next couple of hours."

The rain drummed on the side of the barn more loudly. Thunder exploded overhead. Matt arched his brow.

"You might be stuck here a little while."

Grace tugged the coat closer around her. Harriet must have known how this would go. She'd planned it all. There might not even be a mare in the throes of foaling. She walked down the aisle and peered into the stall. A horse stood, dozing, his lip hanging, his eyes half-closed. He seemed not to hear the wrath of God presently descending on the barn.

Matt looked up from his food. "Next stall."

She walked a little further. A horse lay on a bed of straw, a sheen of sweat covering her flank. Grace drew a sharp breath and lifted her hand to her lips. The mare sighed, her muscles tightened and slowly eased. Grace watched. Transfixed. She didn't know for how long, but she couldn't look away.

Suddenly she felt Matt behind her. The raging storm had drowned out his footsteps. She gasped with surprise.

"Shh," he said. He slipped his arm around her waist. "It's all right."

It had been days since they'd touched, and his embrace drew a small murmur of pleasure from her. She allowed herself to lean back, to seek more of his warmth. He set his other hand on the stall door, caging her in his arms. She closed her eyes, reveling in his touch. For a moment, she was lost in a swirl of emotions.

A noise from the mare drew her attention. She opened her eyes and watched as the mare struggled to bring forth her foal. The mare made a low noise. The foal's legs emerged. With another effort the foal's head appeared. Grace gripped Matt's hand. She held her breath, hardly daring to breath. The mare groaned, stiffened and the rest of the foal was delivered.

Grace's eyes stung as they filled with tears. "Matt..."

He tightened his hold on her but said nothing.

The mare lifted her head and peered behind her. A low rumble came from her chest. She rose and sniffed the foal. Grace watched as she licked her baby. Over the next half hour, the foal struggled to stand. Finally, it stood, swaying on impossibly slender legs. It took a few wobbly steps to his mother's side and nursed.

The rain pelted the windows. Matt moved his hand to the curve of her waist and coaxed her around to face him. He loomed over her, regarding her with a bemused expression.

"Gracie, I might be a little rougher than what you'd like, but I run this ranch the way I see fit."

"I know that."

He had a hand set on either side of her and held her right where he wanted her. Standing so close to him overwhelmed her thoughts, scattering them like dry leaves on a windy Boston morning. His scent invited her closer. The smell made her think of summer sunshine, hard work, leather and something that was distinctly his own scent.

"Why are you worried about me carrying a gun, or busting one of my men?"

"Well... I don't know how to answer." She lifted her chin. "I don't want to answer."

He smiled. "Gracie..."

"I need to think about my answer, that's all."

He chuckled.

She curled her hands into tight fists. "You don't get to just-"

Lowering, he captured her mouth with a kiss, effectively silencing her. His lips were warm and firm. He wrapped his arms around her, pressing her against his powerful build. Clasped in his arms she felt helpless, yet at the same time safe. Her fears seemed to try to taunt her. Baseless things that faded away.

He nuzzled her neck. "Gracie, if you can't tell me, who can you tell?"

"I don't know the answer to that."

"You don't really believe I'd hurt you, do you?"

She lowered her eyes. "You're kind and gentle with me and Abigail."

"Of course."

His voice, a low rumble deep in his chest, felt like a warm blanket on a cold night. Soothing. Comforting. She rested her forehead against him. He stroked her back and brushed a kiss across her temple.

"My father..." her words faded as her courage faltered.

He waited.

She drew a deep breath and forged ahead. "My father, at times, would take to drinking. The accident left him in terrible pain. He'd grow bitter and violent."

A low growl rumbled in Matt's throat.

"He didn't mean it. Ever. And he was so ashamed."

"Of course."

"We all..." A sob welled up in her throat. "We all were ashamed. We never spoke of it, and yet the fear and the shame hung over all of us."

"Sweetheart, I'm so sorry." He cupped her chin and tilted her head. "I am yours, Grace. Always. I'd rather die than hurt you. I plan on showing you that, every day. Until death do us part. I'll give you anything you want, but you won't run things on our ranch. You won't get me to back down, because I protect what I love."

She nodded, unable to reply. He smiled, brushed his thumb along her jaw and gently kissed her lips.

Chapter Thirty-Six

Matt

Matt stayed in the barn till almost midnight, tending to the mare and foal. The storm abated, and by the time he returned to the house, it had drifted south. He crossed the barnyard, casting glances towards the southern horizon. Lightning forked the distant sky. Far off thunder rumbled across the dark summer night.

The rain had been a good thing. Everything had turned brown and desperately needed a good drink. Even more important, the rain had brought Gracie to the barn, and had kept her there, and for that he was glad. Very glad. He hated that she'd suffered. It troubled him, made him want to curl his hands into fists and destroy something. Maybe he was too rough after all. Maybe Grace's fears were well-founded. Maybe his scars weren't the worst of him.

He returned to the house. With each step he battled his doubts, wrestled his demons and whispered a fevered prayer for redemption. He ascended the steps, one by one. He listened for the evening sounds he'd grown accustomed to hearing. Grace's step on the creaking floorboards. Abigail's soft sigh as she fell asleep on Grace's shoulder. Every single sound had grown to mean more to him than he could explain.

Holding his breath, he pushed the bedroom door open.

Grace sat up in bed, her arms folded across her chest. A lamp burned beside her, casting shadows across her features. She knit her brows and shook her head in disapproval. He shut the door behind him, leaned against it and studied her, trying to fathom her mood. She appeared stern, but the corners of her mouth twitched with a barely suppressed smile.

He pushed off the door, went to the wash room to get ready for bed. As he passed the bed and her bedside table, he glimpsed a stack of letters. They were her letters to John, the notes she'd sent from Boston. He'd forgotten that several of them hadn't been opened.

He washed and changed into his bed clothes. On his way to the bed, he snatched the pile of letters. Grace gave a huff of indignation.

"Give those back," she demanded.

He got into bed and waved the letters in the air. "I want to know what you wrote."

"So you can tease me."

"No, sweetheart, because I love you, and because I love you, I want to know everything about you."

Her expression softened. "If I'd written to you, would you have taken the trouble to read them?"

"I would have read them over and over."

Her eyes watered. While he didn't like the notion of bringing tears to his wife's eyes, he loved the way she looked at him now. He wanted to reach for her and show her his feelings with a slow, lingering kiss. He sensed that something passed between them and waited for a sign from her.

"Truly?" she asked. "You would have read them over and over?"

"I would have read them a hundred times," he said softly.

A smile tugged at her lips.

"You see," he said. "I'm not always a ruffian."

"I know that. You're always tender with me, and Abigail. And even with Caleb."

He grimaced. "Caleb! My patience with that boy should earn me a place in heaven."

"Matt, you know that boy is a prize. He's the smartest boy I've ever met."

"Maybe, but he's a rascal."

Matt adjusted his pillow and put his hands behind his head.

"Read me the first letter."

She looked horror-stricken. "No, I can't. They'd sound so foolish."

He grumbled and narrowed his eyes, feigning an angry expression. "You vowed to obey me."

"You read them."

"Fine. I can do that." He motioned for her to come to him and when she'd settled next to him, he pulled her closer. Then he took the first letter out of the envelope. The small lock of hair tumbled out, falling to the blanket.

She picked it up and tucked it back in the envelope.

"You wanted to show off your pretty hair," he muttered.

She shrugged a shoulder. "Maybe."

"Everything about you is pretty. Stop distracting me so I can read this letter."

He opened the letter, with some difficulty since he held one arm around Grace.

Dear Mr. Bentley,

This letter is in response to your advertisement in the Boston newspaper. I am writing to ask for your consideration. My name is Grace O'Brian. I am five foot four and weigh a hundred and fifteen pounds. I am almost twenty-one. I work in a lace-making shop. I am of sound mind and body. My friends and acquaintances say I am pleasant looking. My employer says I am a hard worker.

I hope that you will consider me as a possible wife to you and mother to Abigail.

Respectfully,

Grace O'Brian.

For a long moment, she said nothing. "I can hardly stand to hear the words I wrote read aloud."

Seeing her discomfort, he set the rest of the letters aside and put out the lamp. He'd read them some other time. Perhaps. He didn't like the idea of making her cringe.

"I love your letters." He returned to the bed and pulled her into his arms. "They weren't for me, but they brought you to me, and for that I'm grateful. I have you, Gracie. A wife I never imagined."

She turned in his arms. "I didn't imagine you either, Matt. I thought I was coming as a replacement. A poor substitute."

He stroked her hair, cupped the back of her head and kissed her lips. "You're no substitute. You're one of a kind. You're mine now, Mrs. Bentley. Mine now. Mine tomorrow. Mine forever."

Chapter Thirty-Seven

Grace

Abigail sat in her chair, watching intently as Grace rolled out the pie dough. She smiled as Grace cast her a loving look. After her sweet smile she performed her latest trick, something Matt had taught her – how to blow a kiss.

Grace laughed softly. "Such a clever girl."

The kitchen door opened, and Harriet hurried in. "Gus is waiting to take me to my sister's. Oh, look at you, making a pie while I'm gone. One day I'll find out the secret to your crust, Gracie, you wait."

Grace gave her a look, feigning innocence. "It's nothing secret, Harriet."

Harriet narrowed her eyes, but her response was interrupted by the smacking sound of Abigail's kisses. The small girl gazed up at Harriet, tapped her palm to her lips and blew kisses. Harriet burst into laughter. "You little darling. As much as I love my sister, I can hardly stand to be away from you."

"When will you be back?" Grace asked.

"I'll have Gus fetch me at noon tomorrow. I'll be home to cook supper."

"We'll miss you."

Harriet made a face. "And I shall miss you, but I should go. My sister will have a fit if I'm not there by nightfall."

Grace nodded and watched as Harriet gathered a few things in the kitchen. A jar of jelly, a pie she'd baked that morning and a loaf of bread. A moment later, the woman was gone, the kitchen strangely silent in her wake.

Grace went back to her task. "You miss Harriet?"

Abigail made a sad face. Grace couldn't tell if the child understood or not, but believed that Abigail did, in fact, miss the woman.

Harriet lent a warmth and vigor to the house. Whenever she left, everything seemed dull. And the house seemed especially lonely when Matt was away.

Her skin warmed as she thought of how he'd ridden by an hour ago. He passed the house and, when he glimpsed her, he had touched his fingertips to his lips. It was his way of blowing her a kiss. A small gesture he'd make when he saw her from afar. The kiss was a tender moment that existed just between the two of them, and it never failed to melt her heart.

The back door opened and slammed shut. She wondered if Harriet had forgotten something. It had to be her since Matt had ridden to the back pastures with Luke and the cowboys. Heavy footsteps sounded in the hallway. The hair on the back of her neck rose. She let out a soft huff of surprise. Her panicked gaze wandered to Abigail. The baby gazed at her, wide-eyed.

Grace shook her head, silently willing the child to remain quiet.

"Uh-oh."

Grace shook her head to silence the girl. Abigail frowned. The footsteps moved closer. A chill drifted over Grace. The door pushed open. A stranger, a man, stepped inside.

It was the man from the alley. Jed Sanders. Over the past few weeks, the men had grown more certain he was dead. He stared at her, his eyes lit with a wild look. Blood stained his sleeve a dark copper. A stench of sweat and blood filled the air.

He bared his teeth like a mad dog. “Been looking for you.”

His voice rasped. Abigail whimpered. His gaze drifted to the girl and for a long terrible moment, he stared at the child.

“Leave her,” Grace whispered. “Leave her be.”

He sneered. “Is this Bentley’s kid? I got a bone to pick with him. That’s why I’m here. Best way to hurt a man is hurt what he loves.”

Cold dread washed over her. Without any conscious thought, she put herself between the man and Abigail. The icy fear gripped her. Instead of her usual fearful response, something else took hold. A primitive instinct burned through her. Raw fury misted her sight with red. He might try to hurt her, but she wouldn’t allow him to touch the baby.

“Look at you,” he scoffed. “Little scrap of a girl. Where’s your man now, missy?”

“He’ll be back soon.” She spoke quietly. “You should go now while you have a chance.”

He shook his head. “You think you can run me off?”

His face twisted with an evil smile as he drew closer. He stopped half a pace from her and let his lecherous gaze drift over her face and down the front of her dress. Revulsion burned inside her. Abigail began to cry in earnest. Her fearful weeping tore at Grace’s heart.

“First I’ll take what I want from you. Then I’ll make that brat shut up.” He grinned, showing his yellowed teeth. “For good.”

Grace shook her head.

“No?” he asked in a mocking tone. “Who’s going to stop me? Her daddy?”

"No," Grace said softly.

Confusion flickered behind the man's eyes. A dog barked somewhere in the barnyard. The man jerked his head toward the window. He didn't notice the small movement Grace made as she grasped the rolling pin.

"Her father won't stop you," Grace whispered. "But her mother will."

Grace swung the rolling pin. She struck the man on the side of the head. He grunted. He staggered, gaped at her, his eyes burning with rage.

"You little..."

Grace swung as he lunged forward. The wood connected with his head once more. He swayed, pulling his lips back into a vicious snarl. Again, she swung the rolling pin, this time striking his jaw. The blow made his head snap back. He staggered back, recovered and stood facing her, swaying like a sapling in a storm. He fell to his knees.

Grace darted in front of Abigail. She clutched the rolling pin and kept her gaze fixed on Jed Sanders. Blood flowed from his head. Behind her, Abigail screamed. Distantly, Grace heard the approach of hoofbeats. Jed lifted his hand, reached into his jacket as he stared at Grace. He pulled a knife out. Before he could act, Grace brought the rolling pin straight down, striking the top of his head.

Jed toppled, like a felled oak, crashing to the floor and upsetting two chairs as he went down. Grace watched and waited. Gripping the rolling pin, she moved to where the man lay. His eyes were glazed. Lifeless. Abigail's wails filled the kitchen. Grace didn't make a move toward the child. Instead, she stood over the man, waiting for any sign of life. She was certain he was dead, but others had been certain he was dead before too. She would take no chances.

How much time elapsed, she couldn't tell, but slowly, Abigail's crying softened into a snuffled weep. In the stillness of the afternoon, Grace heard the approach of a horse. She kept her gaze fixed on the man, unable to look away. Matt burst into the house, shouting for her. He stormed into the kitchen, gun drawn.

At the sight of Matt, Abigail quieted.

Matt's eyes widened as he stared at the man lying on the floor. Slowly, he holstered his gun. He took Abigail from her chair, went to Grace, eased the rolling pin from her tight grip and pulled her into his arms. The feel of his strong arms encircling her made the last of her strength fall away.

"I had to do it, Matt," she said.

"I know, sweetheart."

"I didn't want to. But then he told me he was going to hurt Abigail."

"You did the right thing. You're braver than you know." He stroked her head and pulled her close. "Love makes us strong."

Abigail sniffled and patted Grace's face. Grace kissed the child's hand, let out a trembling sigh as her vision darkened and she sank in his embrace.

Chapter Thirty-Eight

Matt

Matt rode to town with Thomas. The two men drove the buckboard to the undertaker to deliver the body of Jed Sanders. For most of the ride, Matt sat silently, trying to come to grips with the terrifying danger Grace had faced all alone. The thought pained him like nothing he'd ever imagined. His wife had fought off Jed Sanders without him or anyone else. He grimaced.

He wished Thomas would put the horses into a trot, but he knew his brother. Out of respect for the dead, even the likes of Jed Sanders, he would keep the team at a steady pace. Jed might have been a murderer, and Thomas might be ruthless when it came to outlaws, but his brother always treated the remains of outlaws with deference.

Thomas gave him a wry grin. "Doin' okay, there Matt?"

He scrubbed his hand down his face. "Never thought I'd see something like that."

"C'mon, now. I know you seen a dead man before today."

"Not one killed by my wife. Jed had a hundred pounds on Gracie." Matt tried to shake off the thoughts of what could have happened. The memory of her trembling in his arms wrenched his heart. The sound of Abigail's cries rang in his ears, casting a chill over his skin.

"The good Lord was watching over Grace," Thomas said. "And Abigail too."

Matt nodded. "I'm mighty grateful."

"Course you are. We all are. Let me tell you something that'll put a smile on your face."

"I doubt there's anything you can tell me that'll make me smile. Not after what I saw tonight. I don't feel like smiling, anyway. All I want to do is get the body to the undertaker and get back to Gracie."

"Gracie's fine. Gus and Caleb are at the house, and Luke will be along soon. She's got plenty of menfolk watching over her."

Matt grumbled. He wanted to be the one watching over Gracie, but Thomas had needed another man for the trip into town. Neither Gus nor Caleb were suited although Caleb dearly wanted to accompany his father on an official, lawman's task. Matt brooded, wishing the trip would go more quickly, yearning to feel Gracie in his arms. He wanted to hold Abigail too. He yearned to tell her he'd always do everything he could to protect her even though he hadn't been there that afternoon. His chest filled with dread once more.

"Stop it," Thomas said.

"What?"

"You're imagining the worst. It won't do you any good, and more importantly, it won't do Grace and Abigail any good. I can see, plain as day, that's what you're doing because I do it too."

"You're not married."

"But I'm a father. Caleb might not be my own flesh and blood, but he's my son. I worry about him. I fret about all the bad things in the world, the mishaps that might befall him. Lately, he's talking about being my *deputy* in a few years."

Despite the somber mood, Matt found his lips curving into a smile. Caleb looked up to his father. Thomas could do no wrong in Caleb's eyes.

"I feel the same way about Abigail. I fret about her too even though I'm her uncle, not her father." Matt rubbed the back of his neck. "It's unsettling."

Thomas chuckled. "It is unsettling. Quit carrying on and listen up."

"Go ahead."

"Baron Calhoun put up an offer for the capture of Jed Sanders."

Matt scoffed. "Aw, c'mon. Baron Calhoun? He wouldn't give up one red cent if his life depended on it. He's the most tight-fisted man I've ever met."

"Calhoun got married. He's a changed man."

Matt grunted. "He married? Probably some rich debutant from Houston."

"Nope. He married the last girl you'd expect. You'd hardly recognize him. The other day I saw him *smiling*."

"You probably mistook him for someone else."

Thomas grinned. "He came to my office. Told me he didn't like the notion of an outlaw skulking around Magnolia. He didn't want to upset his new wife. Then he told me he wanted to offer a thousand dollars reward for Jed Sanders. Dead or alive."

Matt let out a bark of laughter. "Are you telling me my wife is getting the reward?"

"That's exactly what I'm saying."

Matt shook his head at the notion of his sweet, demure Gracie getting a reward for taking down a thug like Jed Sanders.

They turned up the road, over the ridge and Magnolia came into sight. A rush of gratitude flowed through him. They wouldn't need to linger in town. In a quarter of an hour, their business would be done, and they'd return to the ranch. He yearned to be home, to catch a glimpse of Abigail, sleeping in her crib. He ached to be with Gracie, to hold her as she drifted to sleep.

"I wonder if Faith will still want to marry me," Thomas said, interrupting his thoughts.

"Why wouldn't she?"

"Grace could send the train fare herself, from her reward money. Faith wouldn't need my money, or me."

"She's coming to get married. I'm sure of that. I offered to send both sisters train fare. They told Gracie they didn't want my charity."

Thomas looked solemn. "I've been a bachelor so long. I hope I'm not too rough-mannered for a Boston lace-maker."

Matt said nothing. He knew his brother had been hurt before, his trust broken by a woman who hadn't been true to him. Caleb's mother came into the marriage, deceiving Thomas with every word. She'd left the marriage, dying after giving birth to a boy fathered by another man. She'd hurt Thomas. Badly. And she'd hurt Caleb too.

Matt prayed the boy would never find out the truth. He added another prayer that Faith could heal Thomas's shattered heart and that his brother would one day learn to trust again.

They turned into the town of Magnolia, drove to the undertaker's office and finished the task of delivering the outlaw. Matt felt a weight lift from his shoulders as he turned the buckboard around. He snapped the reins. The horses picked up the pace, as if sensing his need to return. Thomas chuckled but said nothing.

"I don't see what's funny," Matt grumbled. "No dead man to fall off, and I want to get back."

Chapter Thirty-Nine

Grace

Abigail wept softly as Grace paced the floor. Grace held her in her arms, whispering soft words to soothe the frightened child. She'd been trying to settle the child for over an hour. At times, Abigail would quiet down, and sink in her arms, her small breaths puffing against Grace's neck. She seemed to drift into sleep, but when Grace tried to lower her to the crib, Abigail would startle and resume weeping. Grace would have to start all over.

Grace felt exhausted. Part of her wanted to cry too, but she refused to feel sorry for herself. The appearance of Jed Sanders, standing in her kitchen, three steps from Abigail, had been the most frightening thing she'd ever known. She'd hardly been aware of her response to him. She barely recalled picking up the rolling pin. It was as if something had taken hold of her, directing her to defend Abigail in a way she could never have imagined.

As she paced the floor, the terror crept back into her heart, but she banished the cold dread, driving it from her thoughts. Instead, she whispered prayers of gratitude, thanking God for keeping Abigail safe. When the terror faded, she hummed a song her mother used to sing. The soft melody settled the child better than any words Grace might have offered. Abigail would quiet down, but not for long.

After the third time she tried to put Abigail in her crib, she heard footsteps on the stairs. Abigail did too. She seemed to know the footfalls belonged to Matt and began to cry with renewed distress. She reached her hands to the door as if willing Grace to seek out Matt.

Before Grace could move to the door, Matt pushed through, a frown on his face.

"What's this all about, Ducky?" he said softly.

Abigail squirmed in Grace's arms, reaching for her father.

Even with Abigail's cries, Grace found herself smiling at Matt. He came to her side, kissed her temple and took Abigail into his arms. The child quieted. Matt's lips quirked. Grace let out a weary sigh and sank into the rocking chair.

This wasn't the first time Matt had helped Gracie settle Abigail. Somehow, the tall, powerful cowboy, who drove hundreds of cattle across rough terrain, and gentle rogue stallions in open fields, could somehow whisper soft words and soothe a distraught child. Grace listened as Matt told the girl about working on the ranch.

"As a Bentley," he began, as he always did, "you'll have to pitch in. Me, your Uncle Luke, your Uncle Thomas, and your father too, we all got our first cow pony when we were just knee-high to a grasshopper. I can see you already, my sweet Abigail, my little Ducky, riding a pretty little roan."

Abigail rested her head against his shoulder as he spoke. Matt smiled at Grace. In the soft light of the lamp, he looked more handsome than she'd ever known. Her heart leapt. Her breath caught. He walked slowly, back and forth, the floorboards creaking beneath his dusty boots.

"Unless you want something fancy," Matt went on. "Like a little dapple grey. Might have to go to Fort Worth to find something as fine as that, but I'd do that for my little girl. We could get you a little saddle. Some boots. Maybe a pair of chaps if your mother will let me."

Grace laughed softly. Matt's words never changed very much and always had a slight teasing lilt. It was very unlikely that Abigail understood very much but she was always comforted by his rendition of her working on the family ranch.

He went on, telling Abigail about child-sized lassos, small gloves and diminutive cowboy hats, all things he intended to buy her. She'd be working so hard as the youngest Bentley cowgirl, the only Bentley cowgirl, she might need *two* ponies. This was the part of the story where Grace always wondered if Abigail might prefer not to spend her days riding across a dust-choked ranch. She might prefer more feminine pursuits. Matt always scoffed at the notion. He'd brush her ideas away, grin and tell her Abigail would be the finest ranch hand he'd ever had.

After Matt finished his story, he settled Abigail in her crib. As usual, the child didn't stir, or make a sound whatsoever.

Matt took the lamp in one hand, grasped her hand in the other, and led her quietly out of the nursery and down the hall to their room. He washed and returned quickly. Grace sat on the edge of the bed. She lifted her hands, held them in front of her, palms up, as if offering an unseen plate.

"Up until today, these have been the hands of a lace maker."

Matt gazed at her without speaking. Lamplight cast a glow across his scars. The smooth, unscarred side of his face was shadowed, but the light flickered across the uneven skin.

"After today," she whispered, "they're the hands of-"

"No," Matt said. "I know what you want to say."

The terrible word that described something she'd never imagined, seemed to stretch between them. It hung in the silence, defining a moment in her life that changed her forever. It wrapped around her soul and made her too afraid to imagine her day of judgement.

Matt came to the bedside and knelt before her. He took her hands in his. Even in the lamplight, his tanned skin was a stark contrast to her pale hands. His hands were rough and calloused. In Boston, her hands had been toughened by her lace work. Here in Texas, the skin had become softer despite the long days she toiled caring for Abigail and their home. He rubbed his thumb across her palm, sending a shiver along her spine.

He gazed into her eyes. "Do you recall when I told you about my scars, how I got them and how I thought they were a sign of being unlucky."

She gave a weak smile as she recalled their first days together. Their conversations had been laced with suspicion, and at times, rancor. That time seemed so long ago, and she was grateful the rancor was behind them. Her heart warmed as a surge of love overwhelmed her senses.

"I remember that day," she said.

"Well, now that you're here, I can't imagine ever feeling unlucky again. I think my scars are the luckiest thing I have. Without these scars my life would have been very different, and I might never have met you."

She blushed.

"You did something heroic today, Gracie. You did something you never imagined you could do." He wrapped his hands around hers, dwarfing them with his size and strength. "We all carry that possibility inside us, the chance to protect someone else. We never know when. Or how. But that's what it means to love another person. You become something better than you were before you loved. Braver. Stronger."

Her eyes prickled with tears.

"I love you, Gracie Bentley," he said, his eyes shining.

"And I love you, Matt Bentley."

"Both of us love Abigail and there's a reason we found each other." He got to his feet, still holding her hands. "The good Lord put us together. We might not understand why, but everything happens for a reason."

He lowered to kiss her cheek.

She closed her eyes, relishing the feel of his kiss. After he released her hands, he put out the lamp, circled the bed and got under the blankets. She went to him and let him fold her into his embrace.

"There isn't anything I wouldn't do for you and Abigail," Matt said as he stroked her back.

Grace smiled. She intended to reply with words that expressed the very same sentiment, but a tiny flutter tickled her low belly. She drew a sharp breath and waited. The sensation returned a little stronger this time. She jerked her hands to her stomach, letting out a small cry of surprise.

Matt sat up abruptly. "What's the matter? Are you hurting?"

The flutter returned.

"Oh," Gracie murmured. "My goodness."

"It was too much for you today wasn't it. It's my fault. I should not have gone to the back pasture. I shouldn't have left you and Abigail."

A soft huff escaped her lips. The flutter grew to something stronger. She waited, barely breathing.

"Gracie," Matt pleaded. "What is it?"

His tone drew her from her reverie. “It’s fine, Matt. It’s more than fine. The baby. I felt her move.”

In the darkness, she could see little, but sensed him moving over her as if shielding her from an unseen threat. A rumble echoed in the quiet. The mattress dipped beside her as he caged her with his body.

“It’s okay, Matt,” she said with a soft laugh. “It’s just a little movement. It caught me off guard.”

“You kinda scared me, Gracie.”

Grace smiled at his rough, protective tone. The events of the day had been hard on everyone. Matt had suffered as much as she had, maybe even more so. “I’m sorry. I hadn’t expected to feel the quickening just yet, although Mrs. Patchwell said it was time.”

“Is that unexpected? Should I go get Mrs. Patchwell? I can saddle up and ride to her sisters and bring her back if you like. I’ll do anything you like.”

Gracie bit back her smile. “It’s fine. Don’t fret.”

Matt groaned. “How can you say that?”

Grace felt another flutter. She reached for Matt’s hand and tugged it to her stomach. She heard his breath hitch. For a long moment he didn’t breathe.

The tiny flutter returned drawing a sharp gasp from Matt.

“There she is,” Grace whispered. “Saying hello.”

Matt laughed. “Hello, sweetheart.”

His tone, soft and gentle, was one he reserved for her and Abigail. The sound of it sent a rush of emotion through her. The tiny prickle in her eyes returned, bringing tears. They pooled in her eyes until they overflowed and rolled down her cheeks. She didn’t wipe them away. She simply let them fall.

“Hello, little girl,” Matt said. “Unless you’re a little boy. Either’s fine. We’re just happy you’re on your way. Your mama's the bravest, best, most beautiful woman I know. And one of the richest."

Grace didn't respond. She just pushed deeper into Matt's arms.

"One thousand dollars rich."

"What?"

"A lot of people wanted that man dead, and as a thank you they want to give you one thousand dollars."

"Ok." Grace felt heavy and tired. She didn't want to think about what had happened that evening, or any reward, or anything to do with that vile man. She just wanted to sleep.

Matt rubbed her stomach, stopping when the tiny sensation returned. "I think I felt something."

"That was it," Grace whispered.

Matt didn't move away, remaining crouched over her and murmuring his amazement with each tiny movement. Finally, the flutters stopped.

"She's gone to sleep," Matt said.

Grace could hear the smile in his voice. He lay down beside her and gathered her close. They lay together in the stillness. Resting in the circle of his arms, Grace drifted to sleep. Her final moments before falling into a deep slumber were tender words from Matt, telling her what a blessing she was to him. An undeserved blessing.

"You're *my* Grace," he said. "More than I ever hoped for."

"And you," she replied, "are the man I always dreamed of but never dared pray for."

They fell asleep, wrapped in each other's arms in the dark of the moonless night.

Epilogue

Eight years later

Matt

Working in his study, Matt heard light, quick footsteps approach his door. There, they stopped, followed by a polite knock on the door. Without looking up from his ledger, Matt spoke.

"Come in."

He smiled to himself, knowing full well who had come to seek him out. Only one member of his family knocked and waited for permission to enter. Abigail. Somehow, she'd picked up impeccable manners despite growing up on a ranch, surrounded by menfolk, not to mention three younger brothers.

Her brothers always forgot to knock. Maybe they were in too much of a hurry, but for whatever reason, Abigail always remembered. She was gentle and considerate and imbued with feminine grace.

He finished adding the numbers from the most recent yearling sale. Once again, the Bentley Brothers Ranch had shown a fine profit. He was grateful, felt blessed and made a note to send a portion of his earnings to the Magnolia school fund, an effort underway to build a school for the growing town.

He closed the ledger and folded his hands atop the leather binding. "Yes, ducky?"

Abigail sat across from him, perched on the chesterfield, giving him a prim look. The last afternoon sunlight made her hair shine. "I think we should get Mama a present."

Outside the window, Matt's middle boy, Silas, scrambled up the pecan tree. John, the eldest boy, gave a war whoop. He danced around the bottom of the tree brandishing his bow and one of the arrows Matt had helped whittle. The tips were dull and harmless, but the arrows flew true. A moment later, John launched one at his brother. A howl came from the depths the foliage.

Matt turned away from the drama unfolding outside and back to his daughter. She ignored her brothers. Instead she kept her gaze fixed on him, determination burning in her eyes.

Matt leaned back in his chair. "I like to buy your mother presents. What do you think I should buy her?"

Abigail smoothed her skirts, a satisfied smile lighting her eyes. "Something very special to make her feel better."

"Is she feeling poorly?"

"Of course she is."

"Why is that?"

Abigail sighed. "Because she had a boy. *Another* boy!"

Matt schooled his features to keep from smiling at her. Andrew, his youngest, came into the world three days prior. It had been an easy pregnancy and delivery, thank goodness. Everyone had rejoiced.

Everyone except Abigail.

She'd made no secret that she desperately wanted a baby sister. She'd even picked out a name – Evangeline. As time went on she added more names: Beatrice, Penelope, Amelia and Alice...

For the last three days she'd let it be known that she was disappointed. And she was sure her momma must be disappointed too. She looked down at the floor and sighed tragically. He could see John in Abigail, his strong will and his ability to negotiate. As stubborn as the day was long, but underneath her steely determination, she had a sweet nature. One that reminded Matt of Abigail's mother, Mary. There was a good bit of Gracie's kindness too.

He'd always imagined Abigail would want to ride ponies and learn a little about the ranch. The girl had no interest in the ranch, however. Almost as soon as she began playing with dolls, she'd set up a little school room in her room. She'd presided over her doll classroom, teaching her dolls how to drink tea and nibble cookies.

Her brothers found her interests bewildering. John and Silas could spend the entire day outdoors and grumble to Mrs. Patchwell about having to come in for dinner.

A sound came from the doorway, an infant's cry. Abigail's eyes widened. "Baby Andrew's crying, Papa."

"I know it. I hear him too."

She jumped to her feet. "We should go see if he's hungry, or wet."

Matt rose and moved to the doorway, gesturing for her to lead the way. Abigail rushed up the stairs. When they got to the baby's nursery, she pushed the door open and hurried to the crib. Matt came to her side and picked up the crying child.

"Hush, now, son. We got you."

The boy quieted. Matt held him close and patted his back. "What do you think I ought to do, Abigail?"

Abigail looked surprised. "Don't you know?"

Matt bit back a smile. "Sometimes I forget. I need a big sister to tell me what Andrew needs."

"I think you should check his diaper. Andrew makes lots and lots of you know...tinkle. Miss Patchwell says he likes to wait for a fresh diaper just so he can make it wet."

"If you think so."

Matt set the boy down on the changing table. Sure enough the diaper was damp. He set about changing the boy into a dry diaper while Abigail stood on a stool next to the table and directed the order of events. When the boy grimaced and began to fuss, she soothed him with a little song Gracie used to sing to her and the boys.

Abigail stroked Andrew's head. The boy quieted and seemed to be calmed by Abigail's touch and her soft melody.

"How long till he smiles?" she asked.

"A couple of months."

"Months?" She looked up at him with a mixture of disbelief and dismay. "Why does everything take so long?"

Matt chuckled. "I suppose that is a long time to wait for a smile."

He carried the baby to the master bedroom. Grace lay in bed, but she was awake and smiling at him. His heart warmed with a rush of love for his wife. She was a little pale, her hair slightly mussed, but he thought she was the most beautiful sight in the world.

Instead of reaching for Andrew, Grace folded Abigail in her arms. "I heard you helping Papa, my sweet girl. I don't know how I'd get by without my darling Abigail."

Abigail wrapped her arms around Grace's neck. "I don't know how you'd get by either, Mama."

Grace smiled up at Matt. He winked back. After Grace told Abigail a few more tender endearments, she patted the bed beside her. "Stay for a little visit, Abigail."

The girl beamed and settled on the side of the bed. Matt gave the baby to Gracie and kissed her on her forehead. Leaving the bedroom, he closed the door gently behind him and went downstairs. He crossed the house, and felt a deep, warm contentment fill his chest.

His life felt full. He had a wife and children when he'd never imagined having either. His home was filled with laughter and joy. As he walked down the hallway, he heard Caleb and Miss Patchwell chuckling. They shared a joke and it was hard to tell who was enjoying it more.

"I'm telling you he was out cold. Completely unconscious." Mrs. Patchwell practically gloated.

Matt stopped at the doorway and sighed. He rubbed the back of his neck as she went on. He'd probably never live this down. When John and Silas had been born, he'd felt a little light-headed. Naturally, the same thing happened when Andrew came along. Matt had merely needed to sit a spell after he'd heard Gracie cry out. If there was one thing he couldn't tolerate, it was Gracie or his children in pain. For that reason, he'd sat down while he waited for the doctor to announce the baby's arrival.

Unfortunately, Mrs. Patchwell had kept him company while he waited. She'd maintained that he'd fainted. Ridiculous. He needed to get off his feet. That's all.

He set his hand on the door, preparing to enter the kitchen when he heard Thomas's laughter join in with Caleb's. Pushing the door open, he found Mrs. Patchwell at the stove stirring a pot. Gus, Thomas, and Caleb all sat at the table.

Gus and Harriet Patchwell had married three years back. Since then, Gus was a constant feature at the kitchen table. Harriet still went by Mrs. Patchwell, saying she'd had the name too many years to change course now. Gus didn't mind.

He was all too happy to be settled with Harriet. He seemed to enjoy being fussed over by Harriet and never complained.

As Matt entered the kitchen, Caleb jumped from his chair and pushed it toward Matt. “You’re looking a little pale, Uncle Matt. Do you need to sit down a spell?”

The group chuckled good-naturedly. Matt shook his head and took the chair from Caleb. In the last few years, Caleb shot up. He was no longer a gangly boy. He was a young man. He carried himself differently, proudly, and managed the cowboys and his responsibilities as well as the other Bentley men. Matt was immensely proud of his nephew. Despite this, he frowned at Caleb, trying to fend off anymore teasing from the young man.

Caleb flashed a broad grin, enjoying every minute of his uncle’s torment.

“I don’t expect I’ll ever hear the end of this, will I?” Matt grumbled.

“Not for a good long while,” Thomas said with a wry grin. “Not for a *very* long while.”

The End

Book Two of Mail Order Bluebonnet Brides

Mail Order Rescue

Texas, 1880 – Cattle rancher Baron Calhoun wants the only girl he can't have. Baron Calhoun wants a son to inherit his lands. He *should* find a wife with money, like one of the rich debutantes in Houston.

Instead, he dreams of a girl he can't have. A poor, shop girl who works at Nelson's Mercantile.

Emily, a girl with violet eyes and fragile smile. She's only nineteen. Far too young for a man of thirty.

Emily hides her heart from Baron along with a dangerous secret. Even worse, her uncle wants to be rid of her. He plans to marry her off as a mail order bride.

Baron won't let anyone threaten the girl he's fallen for. All the money in the world means nothing without Emily by his side.

Books by Charlotte Dearing

The Bluebonnet Brides Collection

Mail Order Grace

Mail Order Rescue

Mail Order Faith

Mail Order Hope

Mail Order Destiny

Brides of Bethany Springs Series

To Charm a Scarred Cowboy

Kiss of the Texas Maverick

Vow of the Texas Cowboy

The Accidental Mail Order Bride

Starry-Eyed Mail Order Bride

An Inconvenient Mail Order Bride

Amelia's Storm

Mail Order Providence

Mail Order Sarah

Mail Order Ruth

and many others...

Sign up at www.charlottedearing.com to be notified of special offers and announcements.

Printed in Great Britain
by Amazon